Unbalanced Accounts

Unbalanced Accounts

KATE GALLISON

LITTLE, BROWN AND COMPANY
Boston   Toronto

FIRST EDITION

THE CHARACTERS AND EVENTS PORTRAYED IN THIS BOOK ARE FICTI-
TIOUS. ANY SIMILARITIES TO REAL PERSONS, LIVING OR DEAD, ARE
PURELY COINCIDENTAL AND NOT INTENDED BY THE AUTHOR.

Library of Congress Cataloging-in-Publication Data

Gallison, Kate.
Unbalanced accounts.

I. Title.
PS3557.A414U5   1986   813'.54   85-24056
ISBN 0-316-30288-0

RRD-VA

Designed by Patricia Girvin Dunbar

*Published simultaneously in Canada
by Little, Brown & Company (Canada) Limited*

PRINTED IN THE UNITED STATES OF AMERICA

Unbalanced Accounts

1

IN MARCH a damp wind blows in Trenton, and it smells of cats. Downtown there are drunks and mad people let out of Trenton Psychiatric, wandering or panhandling in the sun. Nicholas Magaracz, private investigator, passed among them on his way to an appointment, newspapers and snack bags lashing his calves. He was about to do a revolting thing.

Magaracz was going to take a job with the State of New Jersey.

For years (and more and more often) his wife, Ethel, had urged him, "Take a job with the state, Nick. It's a good life, a steady paycheck. You don't have to spend your nights parked outside motels." But the life of a detective was what he wanted. He was his own boss. He got to travel. Last month he had gone to Montreal.

Yet here he was on his way to the Division of Mental Rehabilitation to see his wife's cousin the supervising accountant about a job.

"It isn't like a job as a state worker, Nick," Ethel had said. "Charlie needs a detective. It would only be until you found out what happened to the checks." Magaracz didn't believe her. But they were short of money. Since the legislature passed the new divorce laws, adultery was becoming less and less of a paying proposition.

Industrial espionage was the wave of the future. Credentials in the field were what Magaracz needed. "I'm Nick Magaracz. Maybe you know my work. I cracked the Mental Rehab embezzlement case." As an expert in industrial espionage, Magaracz could put meat on the table until he was ready to retire. Maybe even send Amy to college, if she wanted to go.

The Division's headquarters were in front of him now. Magaracz sighed. Twelve stories high, the building had been erected before living memory. It had changed hands many times but had never been washed. Its last incarnation was as a state office building, and the Division of Mental Rehabilitation occupied most of the floors.

In the days of urban renewal the street in front had been closed to traffic, bricked over, and planted with trees. Still the effect of the Mental Rehabilitation Building — somber, looming — was not softened.

Across the way stood the old Presbyterian church, bright in the spring sunlight. The trees in the graveyard had just begun to bud. Among the headstones of the founders of Trenton a ragged tomcat was slinking and spraying. Loonies and winos sunned themselves on the high curb in front. One of them got up and came toward Magaracz.

"Brother, can you give me some money so I can eat?" the old wino said, cocking a red-rimmed eye. He wore a thrift-shop suit and an asylum haircut, all bristles. Magaracz gave him a quarter and the man shambled back to his companions. Like numb gamblers staring at their slot machines the derelicts gazed out at the building across the street, a great social agency that might yet pay off. The Mental Rehabilitation Agency. Brother, can you rehabilitate me? The great payoff was what they were waiting for, the day when the bells would go off, cherries would come up in the windows, and coins would pour out the front door, or at very least a cascade of golden social workers to put their sad lives right.

But Magaracz was forgetting. There were no services in this building, only record-keeping and accounting functions. Ethel had explained all that. He opened the door to the lobby. All that came out was a wisp of moldy air.

He took one of the small, shaky elevators to his wife's cousin's office on the twelfth floor.

Well fed and darkly bearded, resplendent in a fancy silk tie, classy shirt bulging at the shoulders, and two pieces of a pale gray three-piece suit, Charlie Delpietro was the picture of a middle manager on his way up in the State of New Jersey. This was Ethel's cousin, the supervising accountant of the Mental Rehabilitation Division's Bureau of Fiscal Affairs. He made his pitch to Magaracz.

"The actual position," Delpietro said, "is that of Accountant Two."

"I don't know if Ethel told you this, Charlie," said

Nick Magaracz, "but I don't know anything about accounting."

"Yeah, I know, Nick, but we're dealing with Civil Service regulations here. There's no money appropriated for detectives, but I happen to have this accounting position open, and the list of eligibles expired last month."

"You want me to impersonate an accountant. What happens when they notice I don't know what I'm doing?"

"Nick, it's okay," Ethel's cousin said. "You'll be provisional pending the Civil Service exam, and reporting to me. If you need to look inconspicuous, just take a ledger and an adding machine and start running tapes. By the time anybody notices you aren't a qualified accountant, you'll have found out who took the checks and be long gone. Right? I'll put you in the other corner office, with Stan Green. You'll have a nice big desk, your own phone, everything you need. My girl, Roberta, will do your typing."

"I don't know, Charlie." Magaracz wasn't used to having a "girl" to do his typing, and he didn't own a three-piece suit. One time he tried one on in the store. Ethel said it made him look like her great-uncle Rocco, the one who died in the penitentiary. "I don't know whether I would fit in," Magaracz said. "What if they start asking who's that incompetent bozo?"

Delpietro leaned back in his chair, hooked his thumbs into his vest pockets, and smiled. "Nick," he said, "if I were to walk out in that hall right now and say, 'Who's that incompetent bozo?' in a loud enough voice, it would be just like a fire drill. The whole building would clear out. Trust me. You got nothing to worry about. Do you want some time to think it over?"

"Long enough to go to the men's room, anyway," Magaracz said.

"Be my guest. Second door on your right."

It seemed to Magaracz in the men's room that he could hear music up above his head, the rhythmic thump and buzz of a rock bass line. In the hall he caught a faint whiff that might have been marijuana smoke. Looking around, he noticed a doorway that led to stairs going up to the next floor. Only, of course, there was no next floor. Elevator tower? The cast-iron handrail with its old-fashioned curlicue design must have been original with the building. The stair-way turned a corner, hiding whatever was at the top from Magaracz's view. The radio sounds, if that was what they were, had stopped. Sniffing for smoke, he started up.

As Magaracz turned the corner, feet met his eye, clad in seventy-dollar oil-tanned moccasins, and then muscular legs in designer jeans, and then an equally muscular chest in a fashionable shirt, open to reveal gold chains and hair. The face was that of a faintly insolent weasel.

"Looking for something?" the weasel said.

"Smelled smoke up here," said Magaracz. "Thought something might be on fire."

"Right," said the weasel. "Me, too. So I came up

7

here to check it out. But everything was okay. Nothing is up there. You the fire marshal or something?" He was blocking Magaracz's way completely.

Magaracz backed down a step, and then another. "I'm Nick Magaracz," he said. "The new accountant. And you are —?"

"Freddy Gruver," said the youth, advancing on him. "I'm the mail boy here. What office did they put you in?" They were now at the foot of the stairs. Magaracz stepped back again, and Gruver somehow seemed to expand to fill the whole doorway. "Show me your new office and I'll know where to deliver your mail. Right?"

Magaracz thought: *So he doesn't want me up there.* Later, when Gruver had gone away, he would go up and have a look. Probably he would find, not only the stolen checks, but also several stolen stereos, a color TV, and a cache of dope. "My office is the same as Stan Green's."

"Show me which desk," said Gruver, not moving.

"Another time," Magaracz said. "Got a conference with my new boss." Of course he would take the job. It was too easy to pass up. Whatever was missing around here, this kid took it.

Charlie Delpietro was relieved to hear that Magaracz would take the case. He filled him in on the background of the missing checks while the detective took notes.

The safe was in the bookkeepers' office. It was very old and very big. Here they kept the handwritten ledgers and journals for seven years back. Over the years the Division had moved its bookkeeping offices from one place to another around Trenton, and the safe had to be moved with them. There were fears for the freight elevator cables when the Division had put the accounting offices in their present location on the twelfth floor. Yet the cables had held and the six men from the moving company had somehow not ruptured themselves.

In all those years no one had ever found it necessary to change the combination. Ordinarily nothing of value to anyone outside the Division was kept in the safe. The girls kept their birthday party fund in it, but that never came to more than twelve dollars. Eunice Fogarty, the head clerk, kept the office calculator in it, but only because one of the auditors from the Office of Fiscal Affairs kept borrowing it at inconvenient times.

As for the missing checks, they had been put in the safe only because the substitute mail boy hadn't come around for the afternoon collection.

"Where was the regular mail boy?" asked Magaracz.

"Freddy was in the hospital, having his tonsils out."

"So he's not a suspect," said Magaracz, his heart sinking.

"'Fraid not, Nick. The cops have three witnesses who saw him out cold in the hospital the night the checks were taken. I think the guy is a crook, myself. But in this case his alibi seems to be unbreakable."

"So the checks were in the safe," Magaracz said.

"Yeah. The bookkeepers lock up the safe when they

go home, or if they all have to leave the office for some reason, but the rest of the time it just stands open so they can get at the books when they need to. And why not? To my way of thinking, they don't even need a safe for that stuff. When we moved up here I wanted to get just a bookcase, and let the safe go. Do you have any idea what it cost us to move that thing? But Eunice Fogarty said, no, these were irreplaceable confidential records. We couldn't have just anybody coming in here at night and reading them. To say nothing of preserving them in case of fire.

"And the bureau chief backed her up. So I have a mental picture of this fire, Nick, where the whole building burns down, and when they go to sift through the ashes they find the safe, with all of Eunice Fogarty's records inside, completely unharmed.

"But in any case, this cast-iron monster safe was opened two weeks ago by someone who knew the combination, someone who presumably knew that these checks happened to be in the safe. That's the worst of it, Nick, that it had to be one of my people. We put stops on all the checks, so the bureau isn't out any money. None of the checks have been cashed. It's what it's doing to office morale.

"Most of these bookkeepers have worked for the State of New Jersey for fifteen or twenty years. Some of their mothers work here. Take Ella Peterson. She's sixty-nine years old. When the police asked her if she knew anything about the checks she nearly had a stroke right there. She wouldn't take a paper clip. None of them would. Or anyway, that's what I thought."

10

"How many bookkeepers are there?" Magaracz asked.

"Six. Then there's one other accountant — Stan Green, that is — and my secretary, Roberta, and me. That's all that's up here. Ultimately I'm responsible, being as I'm in charge. It isn't good for my career. The *Star-Ledger* wrote it up. Did you see the article? It made me look bad, Nick."

"You have the combination to the safe?" Magaracz asked him.

"No. I never needed it. If I need to know something I ask Eunice. She has the combination, and one of the others has it, Rose Petrowski I think, so the girls can get into the safe in case Eunice is sick. Of course, any one of them could know it, as well as anybody who ever worked in the bookkeeping office for the last sixty years, since it hasn't ever been changed."

For a moment Magaracz sucked the end of his mechanical pencil in silence. Then he said, "I'll need a list of all the suspects and their home addresses, plus anything you can think of about their personal lives."

"Right. I'll have my girl get it together and type it for you," Charlie said, reaching for the buzzer.

"Wait a minute, Char," said Magaracz.

"What?"

"Didn't you mention your 'girl' as a possible suspect? Maybe you'd better not let her know what I'm really doing here."

"Oh. Yeah."

"You can do it yourself."

"Type it?" Delpietro looked uneasy.

"Handwritten is okay."

11

"Myself? I don't even have any paper." He was rummaging in his desk.

"You could use the back of some of those forms," Magaracz pointed out.

"Will that be all right? It seems kind of sloppy."

"Sure," said Magaracz. "You can even do it in pencil." He picked up a pencil from the desk and handed it to Delpietro. It was yellow, with black lettering: "State of New Jersey — Think and Suggest."

"You want to see your office now?" Delpietro offered. "Or you want to grab some coffee?"

Magaracz said, "I want to see the bookkeepers, if it's okay with you. Get a feel for the kind of people they are."

Delpietro looked at his watch. "They're on break now," he said. "They always go down to Janine's Luncheonette at ten o'clock. It's on the first floor."

"Okay, then," said Magaracz. "I'll check them out down there, and get some coffee too."

But first he would check out Freddy's hideout. Sniffing for smells, listening for telltale sounds, Magaracz crept up the iron stairway.

The elevator machinery was there all right, huge gears and cables smelling of old machine oil. There was a floor or platform along one side of the shaft, of stout wooden planking that didn't creak when he walked on it. Between the platform and the gears and motors was a railing. Two separate elevators hung in the shaft, supported from these works. It would be possible, he thought, leaning out and looking down, to fall between them. If you were very unlucky.

12

The walls were grimy. Cleaning people certainly never came up here to do their work. There was no window, but a dangling incandescent bulb in a little cage gave a certain sickly light.

In the corner of the platform an old but clean blanket was neatly folded.

Interesting, thought Magaracz. *A blanket.*

2

THE DECOR OF Janine's Luncheonette had not changed since 1937. Red leatherette and chrome, and three generations of chewing gum stuck to the underside of the tables. The big booth in the corner was where the bookkeepers always sat. Here they were having their coffee and muffins, seven of them: Eunice, Ella, Agnes, Rose, Muriel, Angela, and Deirdre from the fourth floor.

Eunice Fogarty was presiding. As the office's head clerk, she felt that it was her duty to keep order, even when they were on break. To this end she always tried to steer the conversation toward some topic that was light and pleasant. The hard part was that what was light and pleasant to some of the women was to others heavy and full of dread.

For instance, food. Wouldn't you think that showing the girls a magazine picture of a nice nut cake would cheer them up? But no; Deirdre began to moan about how she couldn't stay on her diet with such temptations, and Ella complained in a loud voice that nuts got under her plate.

Rebuffed on the issue of the nut cake, Eunice turned to a page of new hair styles. Deirdre seized upon this as an opportunity to nag her teenaged daughter, the baby of the office, to get her hair up off her face. "See, Angie? If you wore it like this, people could see your pretty eyes."

"Big deal," the girl muttered. Hastily Eunice turned to an article on bridal fashions. But even love and marriage, it seemed, were not universally approved of.

"When are *you* going to get married again, Muriel?" remarked old Ella Peterson to the group's only divorcée.

"When I marry again, Ella," Muriel replied, "I'll have a big wedding in Hell, and you can all come and wear your ice skates, because it will be frozen over."

"Aren't you going to find a replacement for Ed?" said Rose Petrowski, laughing.

"My dear," said Muriel, "Ed could only be replaced by four muggers and a stiff dose of strychnine." She took a savage bite from her English muffin.

Little Angela spoke up in a voice of outrage. "How can you talk like that about someone you shared your life with for fifteen years?"

"Oh, honey, how young you are," said Muriel. It was true, Eunice reflected, that Angela was still in high school last year the time that Muriel tried to jump down the elevator shaft after she heard her son calling his stepmother "Mom." Poor Muriel.

Change the subject again. "Deirdre," said Eunice. "What's new on the fourth floor?" Deirdre had gone downstairs to another office to take a promotion.

"Nothing, Eunice. What's new on twelve? I don't suppose you found those checks?"

15

"Not so far, dear," said Eunice. Another sore subject, this time one that was offensive to Eunice herself. People had been saying that one of her girls took the checks, an unthinkable idea; worse, a notion tending to create disharmony in Eunice's bookkeeping unit.

"Well," said Deirdre, "send me a postcard if you run across them. Ha, ha." "I'll send you a postcard" was a standard embezzlement joke among the bookkeepers, all of whom were painfully overworked, painfully underpaid, and, Eunice was certain, painfully honest. The idea of absconding to some resort island with any of the millions of dollars that passed through their hands was uproariously funny to them.

"Nine thousand dollars," muttered Rose Petrowski. "Much silk. Many bangles. You know, I got a call on those checks this morning."

"Oh, yes?" said Eunice.

"Some nursing home in Atlantic City. The man was pretty nasty."

"Tell me more."

"I picked up the phone," said Rose, pantomiming, "and here was this guy who said he was the business manager of the Boardwalk View Rest Home and where were their checks. Turned out that the Boardwalk View was supposed to get three hundred and seventy-five of those checks, all for different patients, all taken in the theft."

"Didn't he know about the break-in?" said Eunice. She always called it that, though the police insisted that nothing had been broken.

"No," said Rose. "Evidently it didn't make the At-

16

lantic City papers. Those letters were supposed to have gone out Monday telling people about their checks, but it seems Roberta didn't get them copied in time. Probably her nail polish was still wet or something."

"Now, Rose," said Eunice.

"So I had to explain to him," Rose went on, "that he has to sign two affidavits, and that the caseworker from the Atlantic County district office would bring them around, and after that his patients would get their replacement checks next month in the regular check run."

"Right you are," said Eunice.

"Well, he didn't like that. First he said he knew the governor personally. Then he asked for my name and title, which I gave him, and then he wanted to talk to my supervisor, and I said she was in a meeting, which you were, Eunice, and after that he asked me if I knew how great a percentage of his operating expenses those checks represented, which of course I didn't. I mean, who the hell cares? I have my own job to do without trying to do his. Operating expenses."

"Right, Rose," and "You bet," said the women.

Eunice said, "Rose, aren't the checks from that account for personal allowance checks for the patients? How could he use them for operating expenses?"

"Some of them might have been for room and board. Anyway, if you added them all up it would come to quite a lot, almost the whole nine thou."

Agnes said, "Atlantic City. I bet he's a mobster and owes it all for gambling debts."

17

"Maybe that's it, then," Rose said. "A desperate man. Anyhow, the next thing I knew he was talking about how sorry he would be to have to put his patients who were wards of the state out on the street. 'I would *hate* to have to take that step,' he said, in this nasty voice."

"What did you tell him?" asked Eunice.

"What could I say? I'm no social worker. I gave him the phone number of the district office in Atlantic City and told him to call there and talk to the caseworkers. He wasn't happy. He said he needed the checks now, and it would be much better for all concerned if we could find them or replace them at once, and all this crap. Finally I got rid of him."

"Let's hope he doesn't get the idea to come around looking for them," said Ella darkly.

"If he does, you can show him right where Rose's desk is," said Deirdre.

"Thanks, kid," said Rose.

"Maybe we can show him Muriel's desk," Eunice said. "By the time he finds our office, she'll be long gone."

"Spare me," said Muriel. "All I need is angry mobsters on my trail to make my life complete."

"Why should she be gone?" said Rose. "Muriel, where are you going?"

Muriel said, "Girls, I haven't told anyone but Eunice yet, but I'm leaving town."

"Oh, no!" "What will we do without you!" "Leaving town!" "Who will do the *Dedicated Unclaimed Journal*?" the women cried.

18

"I'm afraid the *Dedicated Unclaimed Journal* will have to do without me," said Muriel. "I've got two weeks' vacation pay coming and I have to leave Friday."

"As soon as that?" said Rose.

"You remember my brother-in-law died a short time ago in Boston. Well, my sister has no head for business, and she can't manage at all without him. She needs me to keep store."

The women gave a sort of moo of sympathy.

"In fact, I'm shaking the dust of Trenton from my feet." She smiled.

"Oh, but we'll miss you!" "I can't believe it!" the women said. But Rose said, "I think it's the best thing for you, dear, after all you've been through. You need a complete change of scene."

"I'm looking forward to it," Muriel said. "I mean, I'll miss you girls, and my friends at home and all, but . . . I never really liked Trenton."

"You've had a lot of grief here," Rose agreed.

"You could say that," said Muriel. She glanced over her shoulder at the front window of Janine's, almost as if she expected some further grief to come in the door. What she saw caused her to cry, "It's Ruth Ann! Look out, ladies!"

Eunice followed her gaze and, sure enough, there was her nemesis, Ruth Ann Walker, the bag lady, who used to be her clerk. To encounter Ruth Ann was agony, seeing she had gone so crazy and sunk so low. She mashed her large pale nose against the window and squinted in, distorting the strangely painted flesh

19

of her face against the glass. Her wild black wig was rattier than ever. The two pairs of glasses that she always wore now were knocked awry. She couldn't possibly have seen them.

"Let's go before she sees us," Eunice said, "and tries to sell us those awful hats. I hate to be cruel, but . . ." Hastily the women got up, paid their bills and left.

The woman outside withdrew her face from the window, leaving behind on the glass the print of a scarlet frown. Slowly she moved away.

In the booth next to the corner, Magaracz replaced his notebook in his breast pocket and left a tip for Janine.

The bookkeepers were back at their duties when Magaracz returned to the twelfth floor. The sound of their adding machines could be plainly heard through the door to their office. As he came off the elevator Magaracz caught sight of the panhandler who had accosted him that morning. The old man was headed off down the hall, and indeed he went into the far corner office and closed the door behind him. This was cause for Magaracz to pull out his notebook and write some more.

He felt he had many surprises with which to confront Charlie Delpietro back in his office.

Charlie was indeed amazed.

"Muriel leaving!" He ran his fingers through his hair, frowning. "And on Friday. I'll have to replace her. Why would — after all we — damn it, I bet she's the one who took the checks. Now she thinks she'll make her getaway. I want you to nail her, Nick. What ingratitude. After we were so nice to her the time she tried to kill herself."

"Tried to kill herself?"

"She pretended to try to kill herself is what I always thought," Delpietro said. "It was more like a bid for attention. She was having a hard time and she got a bad phone call, and she ran out in the hall and tried to throw herself down the elevator shaft."

"What hard time was she having?" Magaracz said. "What was this bad phone call?"

"Divorce," Delpietro said, shrugging.

"Ah." Magaracz had dealt with enough hysterical spouses in his time to be able to imagine the cause and the effect. Luckily for his clients, to say nothing of his insurance rates, Magaracz's own office was on the second floor, and his windows didn't open as far as these did. He went over to the window, which was wide open, and put his head out. There was nothing between him and the pavement twelve floors below. "All the windows open like this, don't they?" he said. "Why would she try for the elevator shaft?"

"That was my point," Delpietro said. "The door doesn't open unless the elevator is there, yet here she was clawing at it and yelling that she was going to put an end to her troubles. You can see for yourself how easy it would be if you were serious. No screaming, no carrying on, just climb over the sill and join your ancestors. There isn't even a ledge."

It was true. "Then what happened?" said Magaracz.

"The other bookkeepers grabbed her and calmed her

21

down. Stan Green took the afternoon off and drove her home."

"Anything going on there?"

Delpietro appeared startled by the question, and thought it over for a moment. "Stan is a very prim, shy guy, a typical accountant. He has an attractive wife at home and two daughters."

"Do you know that he is right now closed up in his office with one of the local street bums?"

"One of the local . . . Oh, you mean Leo. That guy is his brother. He comes up here every so often and gets money from Stan, and then he goes off on a drunk. He doesn't really bother anybody. He's probably gone away already, just in the time we've been sitting here talking."

"Leo Green." Magaracz made another note in his book. "So you don't think Stan the accountant is involved with Muriel. What about the other women?"

"I honestly haven't thought about it," Delpietro said. "But I tell you what." He took out a yellow legal pad, with which he had supplied himself when he found that he had no paper. "We'll write all the men on one side, and all the women on the other, and then draw lines. Men: Stan, me, and I guess we have to include that little creep Freddy. Women: Eunice, Rose, Ella, Agnes, Little Angela, Muriel herself, and my girl, Roberta." He gave the pad to Magaracz. "I was never any good at parlor games," he said; "you do it."

"Okay," said Magaracz. "Who do you want to be connected with?"

"They're all either too young or too old for me," Delpietro said.

"Except Roberta," said Magaracz.

"Aw, come on, Nick, give me a break. Sure, I'd like to be connected to Roberta. Anytime. But for one thing, she has this weight-lifter husband, who would take me apart."

"Freddy, then?"

"Freddy would come apart even faster than me. No," said Delpietro, "I guess Freddy has dated every unmarried girl in the building at one time or another — every one under twenty-five, that is — but not Roberta, that I ever heard of."

"Little Angela?"

"Hey, that's right. They were together at the office Christmas party. Right, Nick, we draw a line from Freddy to Little Angela."

"Stan?" Magaracz prodded.

"Dotted lines, Nick. Dotted lines to all of them. Stan and old Ella Peterson under the ledger racks. Nick, I think you're looking into the wrong kind of hanky-panky. The name of the game is theft."

There was a knock on the door and Roberta wiggled in, her arms full of office supplies, in a cloud of good perfume. "Word games!" she said, eyeing the yellow pad in Magaracz's hand. "Can I play?"

"No, honey, this is an accounting game," Delpietro said.

Clumsily Magaracz concealed the chart. "I'm the new accountant," he said. She gave him a dimpled smile.

"I know," she said. "Mr. Maggeraxe, right? I brought this stuff from the supply room for you."

Certainly she was a tasty dish. "Magaracz," he corrected. "It rhymes with 'pots.'" Roberta the secretary was, in fact, so dainty and graceful that she made Magaracz feel like a horse. For a moment he wondered what to do with his hands, then stuck them out and took some of the supplies.

"Well, Mr. Mugger Rots, if you'll step this way, we can get you settled in your new office," she said. He followed her down the hall, watching her step that way. It was interesting.

Stanley Green was at his desk balancing the books when Roberta Schwartz came wafting in with an armload of supplies and put them on the other desk. She said nothing to him. A sigh escaped his lips into the stagnant air of the room. Still Roberta did not speak or turn around, but left, heels and hips twinkling contrapuntally.

"She walks in beauty like the night," Green murmured.

"Certainly does," agreed a voice behind him. Green turned. There stood the new man.

3

NIGHT IN THE office of Nicholas Magaracz, private investigator. Soft sounds of traffic. Striped with light from the venetian blinds, Magaracz sits alone at his desk, observed only by his stuffed fish and sad-faced paint-by-numbers clown.

He is preparing to play a tape.

In the ordinary course of his work, Magaracz needs no more than one tape recorder and microphone. You put it under the bed, set it going, and there's your evidence. But industrial espionage is different.

Delpietro wanted him to bug all the phones.

"What do you think this is, *Mission Impossible?*" Magaracz said to him. "Get me five thousand dollars for equipment and I'll bug all the phones. All I have is this one mike."

He was reduced to moving the microphone around at random and trusting to luck.

What he has here is forty-five minutes of the bookkeepers.

At first, a lot of background noise. Then adding machines, one at a time, several together, several in varying rhythms. Then a sneeze, and a chorus:

CHORUS: God bless you.

BOOKKEEPER 1: It's hot in here, Eunice. Agnes, isn't it hot in here? I think we should turn the fan on.

BOOKKEEPER 2: Hot? Jeez, I'm freezing. Look at me. My lips are blue and I've got two sweaters on already. Muriel over there is sneezing her head off.

BOOKKEEPER 1: Well, I'm sweating to death.

BOOKKEEPER 2: I tell you, my teeth are chattering.

BOOKKEEPER 3 (a small voice close to the mike): Take them out, then.

BOOKKEEPER 2: What?

EUNICE FOGARTY: Quiet, please, girls. I need to concentrate while I'm doing this report.

Click, click, click, ka-shuck, ka-shuck. The sound of adding machines continues. Magaracz is drawing a seating chart. What does he hope to discover, eavesdropping on these women? He doesn't know. In his mind he sees their faces, middle-aged, cheerful, honest he would have said, most of them widows except for the young girl and the desperate divorcée, Muriel Engelhardt. Now there is a likely suspect. A man-hater, and leaving town, too.

Feet approaching, and the door, and a woman's voice.

WOMAN: Good afternoon, Eunice mavourneen.

EUNICE: Good afternoon, Deirdre of the Sorrows. What do you have there for us?

DEIRDRE: Kickouts. Keypunch wants these cards corrected before three o'clock.

EUNICE: They don't want much, do they?

26

DEIRDRE: Now, now, dear, there aren't more than three hundred in this pile.

EUNICE: Well, never mind. Agnes, Ella, take these cards, please, and get busy on them. Idle hands are the devil's workshop.

DEIRDRE: Before I go, Eunice, could you let me have a Mass card? One of the seven-dollar ones, please.

EUNICE: Certainly.

Sound of a drawer opening.

DEIRDRE: My neighbor's mother passed away yesterday, poor thing.

EUNICE: Yes, I saw it in the paper. Was she sick long?

DEIRDRE: She was doctoring for a long time, but nobody thought it was anything very serious. But she fell last week, and broke her hip, and after that she just seemed to . . .

The story of the old woman's painful symptoms and sad death is drowned by the almost tuneless humming of someone closer to the microphone. The sound of the adding machines reaches a crescendo.

BOOKKEEPER (whispering): Shut up, shut up, shut up . . .

Sound of the door closing.

A short discussion follows in which three of the women discuss their hysterectomies. Magaracz comes close to being embarrassed by this. Clearly it is not a conversation for the ears of men. But it subsides, giving way to a long stretch of adding machines, doors opening and closing, shuffling papers, scraping chairs, coughs, and occasional humming and singing. Sometimes two or three of the women sing at the same time, but never the same song.

There is a spirited argument over the correct way to prepare a roast of pork.

Magaracz is wondering afresh how this can possibly get him any farther with his case. Then he notices that something he had taken to be background noise is actually a stifled sound of sniffling and sobbing. No one in the office is paying any attention.

A clue, a clue. But who is crying? The divorcée? The old woman? The young girl? The sound stops in mid-sniff as the tape runs out.

Night too in the Boardwalk View Rest Home for the Disturbed Elderly. Of the 375 patients (all on public assistance) bedded in the Boardwalk View, twenty-two have not yet received their evening medication. Their whimpers and shouts echo in the halls as the night attendant makes her rounds in squeaky crepe-soled shoes. The old frame building creaks of itself, as does the new heating system.

Closing his eyes, Edward Burkhaus Franklin in his office in the tower imagines himself at the helm of some great four-masted slaver, bound for the Bermudas. Through the open window comes the faint slow pulse of the surf.

Franklin leans back in his black leather armchair. He has swallowed a new sample that the pharmaceutical salesman left that afternoon. More and more do the creaks seem to be his ship's rigging, and now he feels the deck begin to heave and swell. He can see the lights of little boats far out over the ocean, or so it seems to him as he waits for the drug to take effect; one can never really be sure.

Presently Franklin closes his eyes, floating. He is beginning to experience a sensation of oneness with the universe. Almost at the same time he feels a bead of saliva dribbling down his chin. He sits up with a start and wipes his mouth.

In the office doorway stands his elder son, Edward Junior. The boy is dressed in his casino-going costume, evening clothes and Adidas running shoes. He looks uncomfortable and tense.

"Dad, I need my allowance," he says. "I was supposed to get the money last week."

"Well, son, as I told you before, we have a fairly serious cash-flow problem this month."

"Did you talk to those people at the State today?" the boy says, pacing and jingling his change. "Have they put a tracer on my checks? What did they say?"

"The checks were stolen," Franklin tells him. "Someone took them out of the safe in the state office in Trenton. The ladies of the state bureaucracy have informed me that it will be another month before those checks can be replaced."

"Shit. I haven't got a month."

"Has your tailor been dunning you?" Franklin asks, having his little joke.

"Never mind," the boy says. "Forget it. It's not

29

important. I owe it to a guy. I can't even go out, if you want to know."

"Nine thousand dollars?"

"I borrowed it," the boy says, shrugging. "He knew I was good for it."

"A loan shark?"

"It's okay, Dad. It's my money, isn't it? If I want to, I can borrow on it. It just happened that a really good opportunity came up, and I needed it sooner than usual."

"And now you can't go out. Well, then. You'll have to stay in. Won't you sit down? Would you like one of these?" Franklin pushes the box of drug samples across the desk toward his son.

"I don't do that shit," says the boy, curling his lip.

"Hm. Well. If you're in all that much of a hurry, suppose you and your brother Hank take a ride to Trenton tomorrow and find out exactly what happened to your allowance. In a quiet way, of course. We wouldn't want to attract any undue attention." He closes his eyes as the room revolves slowly.

4

THE BOOKKEEPERS' office was changed from a colorless place of dull toil to a festive bower of revelry. "Good Luck Muriel" was spelled out in Kleenex flowers Scotch-Taped to the office wall. Red and blue crepe-paper banners hung over the open windows to stream now in, now outward in the breezes. Paper tablecloths were spread over the desks, pushed together to form a vast and sumptuous buffet. Huge platters of cold cuts and cheese, great plastic buckets of potato salad and coleslaw, oceans of punch, mountains of snowflake rolls, foothills of home-made cakes and pies: all this awaited the guest of honor. In flagrant contravention of the office rules, someone had found and lit two candles.

The bookkeepers and their friends from other offices waited for Muriel, clustered against the wall on the two sides of the doorway, trying to act normal and yet not be seen or heard from the hall outside. They made a twittering noise, much like a flock of small birds.

Eunice had sent Muriel on a wild-goose chase to the bank. As soon as she was on the elevator the book-keepers had produced this feast from many hiding places. Out they came: coolers, cookers, trays, bags, boxes, napkins, plates, cups, and precious forks, hoarded from party to party. Decorations went up. In no time everything was ready.

Now they were waiting.

Angela wasn't feeling well.

Crushed against the wall behind two bulky clerks, she thought with longing of the ladies' room. There it would be cool and deserted; there she could sit down, and maybe put her head between her knees, and nobody would ask what was wrong.

"Someone's coming!"

"Is it her?"

"Sh!"

Mr. Magaracz stepped into the room.

"Stand over here and don't say anything," said Rose Petrowski. He moved to the side. The women resumed their chirping.

"Is she coming now?"

"Here she comes!"

"Hush!"

"The elevator door is opening!"

But it was not Muriel who got off the elevator. It was two strange men.

The two came into the bookkeepers' office, unsmiling, wearing cologne and pale silk three-piece suits, their shirts open, their feet in expensive running shoes. The younger one had a thin first growth of sandy moustache. There was something reptilian in the way they carried their heads, long on their necks and slowly swiveling to look at every person in the room.

"They're after me," Angela thought.

That moment was the first inkling she had that everything was going really wrong.

"Is this the accounting department?" said the clean-shaven one.

"Where they make out the checks?" said the other.

"Yes," said Rose. "But, listen, could it wait a minute? We're having a surprise party right now."

"Uh . . . we just need . . . ," said the moustache.

"Here, stand over there. Ella, give them some punch," said Rose.

"Hide! Here she comes."

"Over here! She'll see you."

"Got the camera?"

"I want to see her face."

"There's the other elevator."

"It's her!"

Muriel came in then. The camera flashed, the women all shouted "Surprise!" and Muriel began to cry. The party was a great success.

Out of Roberta the Secretary's office came Charlie D., carrying presents and framed testimonials, followed by Stan Green and Roberta herself. Angela looked up and there was Freddy. She tried to catch his eye but the crowd was very thick. He seemed to be going straight for the food.

Charlie D. called for attention. All during the speech he made the clerks were muttering things, but luckily he never heard them. "People," he said, "today we say good-bye to a girl that we've all enjoyed working with, a girl who has meant a lot to this office, a

33

girl who has been a real hard worker for us for the past five years."

("— worked her butt off for five years and only one stinking promotion for it —")

("— not his fault. Charlie D. has only been here a year and a half —")

("— right. Five years ago he was still in high school —")

"Muriel," Delpietro continued, "we all want to wish you the best of luck. This certificate is to commemorate your five faithful years with the State of New Jersey." He handed her the framed certificate and shook her hand while the flashbulbs popped. "And now I believe Eunice has something for you."

Eunice stepped up with a package in her hand. "Some of us got together, Muriel, to give you this little token. It's just something to remember us by." Blushing, smiling, and sniffling, Muriel undid the bow and held up a jeweler's box.

"Look, girls," she said. "It's my birthstone. How beautiful. Thank you." She blew her nose. "Let me pass it around if you haven't all seen it."

They all lined up for the food then. Angela looked around for Freddy, but she couldn't see him. Maybe he took his cold cuts up in the elevator tower. Maybe he was up there waiting.

Stanley Green had managed to fill up two plates; he offered one to Roberta, sitting on a desk with her legs crossed. She smiled at him, a flash of dimples and perfect teeth.

"Look at herself, grinning in that low-cut dress," said Deirdre.

"She's always smiling," Rose observed.

"Sure," said Angela. "Why not? Handsome, rich husband — she doesn't even have to work — beautiful clothes, gets her hair done every week, fourteen thou a year and all the men in the office drooling all over her. Who wouldn't smile?" There was Freddy, after all, sitting by the door talking to the two strangers. Angela thought, *I ought to warn him.* But of what?

"Does she really make fourteen thousand a year?" said Deirdre.

"I got a look at her W-Two," said Rose. "Fourteen grand for doing her nails and reading *Vogue* magazine. And she wants us to answer the phone when she's out of the office."

"You know," said Eunice, "that girl might have troubles that you and I don't know anything about. You shouldn't be so quick to condemn her." She thrust a plate of cake at Deirdre. "Take this, dear. It's for you," she said.

Deirdre said, "I can't. Weight Watchers meeting tonight."

"You should take your Angela along," piped Ella, cruising up with a plate of cake and a cup of punch. "She's getting quite chubby; aren't you, dear?" Juggling her punch, she pinched the girl's cheek.

That horrible old woman. Now they were all staring at her waist.

"I think she looks fine," said Deirdre, hugging her. The smell of meat on her mother's hands made Angela want to be sick again.

Roberta came over, smiling, passing around the pictures of her trip to the Bahamas. Ella went off to press food on Mr. Magaracz, who was, of all things, taking notes. Moustache and Cleanface were leaning over Freddy with great interest while he described his new van to them.

"That must have set you back plenty," said Moustache.

"I do all right," the mail boy replied.

"Listen to that kid, bullshitting again," said Deirdre. "You ought to hear him with the girls downstairs, bragging about his van, bragging about his apartment."

"Oh, Mother, leave him alone. You're always running him down."

Deirdre gave her a strange look. "Let me tell you something, honey," she said. "See those fancy clothes he's wearing? Designer jeans and the whole bit? Women buy him those clothes."

"That isn't true," Angela said. Surely it couldn't be true. "What women?"

"What's in this punch, Eunice?" said Muriel. "It's delicious."

"Rose made it," said Eunice.

Rose said, "It's ginger ale, pineapple juice, and sherbet. Plus a little oh-be-joyful." She winked. "But we won't let on about that."

"But how do you get the grapes like this?"

"They're frosted."

"Frosted?"

"Secret recipe. You dip them in egg white and roll them in sugar."

Egg white. Oh, egg white made her want to vomit so much. If only she could reach the ladies' room.

"Excuse me," said Angela as she lurched toward the door. The two men were in her way, although Freddy was gone. They turned to leave, but Rose stopped them.

"Are you gentlemen finished with your forks?" said Rose, cheerful but insistent. "We save the forks."

"Oh. Yeah." They gave her their plastic forks, Moustache licking his off first.

"You have a lot of parties?" Cleanface asked.

"Just birthdays and special occasions," said Rose. "Tomorrow is Muriel's last day."

"She's leaving, huh?" said Moustache. "What, did she hit the lottery? Or, like, come into a lot of money?"

"No," said Rose, laughing politely. "She's going to Boston to live with her sister and help out with the store." She lowered her voice. "Her brother-in-law passed away. Poor thing."

"Shame," said Cleanface. "Have a nice day," said Moustache, and the two went out into the hall.

Angela slipped past them, intent on finding a quiet place to throw up her lunch. It wasn't until long afterward that she remembered seeing them turn right, away from the elevators. It might even have been that they went up the stairs. She felt so sick that it was all the same to her.

In a surprisingly short time the debris of the party was cleared away. The women returned to their work. Many accounts had to be balanced before next Tuesday, the end of the month.

Angela, partly hidden from the eyes of Eunice by a

large rack of ledger printouts, was writing names over and over on a piece of journal paper. Angela Gruver. Mrs. Frederick R. Gruver. Mr. and Mrs. Fred Gruver. Sometimes she would make a flourish at the end, or draw the line back under the name again after the *r* and make two crosshatches on it.

She was practicing.

Roberta the Secretary put her head in the office. "Did one of my pictures fall out of the pack in here?" she asked. "I'm missing one."

"Not that I know of," Eunice told her. "We'll look around. Maybe it fell down behind something." Roberta thanked her and went back into her own office.

"I took it," Rose Petrowski said. "I confess. I wanted it for a pinup of her lovely self. I'm going to have it blown up and put it over my desk."

"Now, Rose," said Eunice, "you're just cross because you didn't get to go to Nassau this year."

Rose said, Nassau, her assau.

Roberta went into Charlie D.'s office. She found him conferring with Nick Magaracz.

She said, "Have you been fooling around with my trip pictures?"

"What do you mean, fooling around?" Delpietro said.

"One of them is gone. The one where Barry and I are holding the piña coladas on the Encantador Hotel terrace. It was a terrible picture. You could see that one of my nails was broken."

"That wasn't such a terrible picture," Delpietro smirked. "You were hardly wearing any clothes."

38

"I was wearing resort wear," she said. "That shows how much you know. It's what you're supposed to wear at a resort. It's the *style*."

"You could have fooled me," Delpietro said. "I just thought you were half-naked. So the picture is missing, is it? Want me to go look around the men's room?"

"You're *terrible*," she said, and flounced out.

"She's a good kid," Delpietro said.

Muriel, too, was writing, but on a five-by-eight pad rather than expensive Boorum and Pease bookkeeping paper. For Muriel, the act of wasting a sheet of journal paper when there was cheap foolscap to be had was the sort of behavior to be expected of people from New Jersey and, as such, despicable. It was the sort of thing her ex-husband might do, or teach their son to do. Come on, son, let's cheat on our income tax, let's drop chewing gum in the street, let's waste paper. Let's tell lies to Mother.

If anyone had pointed out to her that the list she was making had nothing to do with her work, and so represented a theft of the time she owed the state, she would have shrugged and replied, "What do you want? This is, after all, New Jersey." But tomorrow she would board the Patriot, that excellent comfortable train, and leave this place behind her. Back home in New England she could be clean and free.

But not too free. As the scenery rushed past the scratched green windows there would be a man, perhaps, in the red plush seat beside her, wearing tweeds, with a nice pipe in his mouth. (She would remember

39

to sit in the smoking car.) She must dress carefully for the trip and make up her face. He would have all his hair. He would have money. He would get off in Boston and they would meet later.

"Good cocktail dress," she wrote on the pad. She was making a list of things she would like to buy.

Stan Green went past the door, carrying his black raincoat and his briefcase (which held, it was said, only his overshoes and lunch). The women knew it must be five of five. Stanley Green always left early to catch his bus. They began to gather their things together.

Muriel headed for the ladies' room to tidy up. In the hall she heard a low voice call, "Hey, lady!" It came from Green's office. She went inside.

The two men were there who had come to her party.

Five o'clock. Magaracz and Charlie Delpietro went down the stairs, while the women waited in the hall for the chance to pack themselves into the tiny elevators. These, when they came, were already crammed with riders from the floors immediately below, who got on and rode up to save a place for themselves, because, as Muriel would have said. this was, after all, New Jersey. Muriel herself was not in the crowd, a fact that went unnoticed at the time. She and Rose Petrowski were supposed to carpool back to Yardville with Eunice.

They waited downstairs for her for quite a while. At last no one was left in the lobby but Eunice, Rose, and Mr. Green's brother the wino, peering at them out of the corner with his crafty red eyes.

"I thought she was on your elevator," Rose said.

"Maybe we ought to go back and look for her," Eunice said. But in the end she went to get the car and bring it around. In so doing, she missed by two minutes hearing Muriel scream, and seeing her fall twelve floors to the brick paving of the Commons.

5

EUNICE WAS dismayed to see that Little Angela had made three big tear stains on the ledgers.

"How can you stand there talking about the Dedicated Unclaimed Fund," the girl said, "when poor Muriel is lying dead?"

Eunice patted her shoulder.

"Honey," she said, "you have to. I remember your mother coming in and doing her work with your poor father lying dead, God rest his soul. That's what you do. You go on.

"Sure, I feel badly about Muriel's death. I don't think there's anybody in this office who isn't asking herself whether there wasn't something we could have done to prevent it. We all feel terrible. She was a good person.

"But it won't bring her back for us to sit here and cry about it, and let the work go. She wouldn't want that. And then we'd have twice as much to do afterwards.

"We'll go to Mass tomorrow, and we'll pray for her soul, poor thing. But right now, I want you to put the penciled totals in the right-hand column, this way. See?"

And so that's what they all did; they went on.

Magaracz went on detecting. He sat at his desk for a long time considering the nature of the scuff marks on his windowsill.

A struggle? With whom? Were there tufts of hair? Buttons? No, no other clues. A mark on the wall that might have been the print of a running shoe, or not. Was it there Friday? Magaracz couldn't remember.

The detective considered for a moment his office-mate, who was reading Saturday's *Trentonian*. A weird bird. He might have been capable of throwing that bookkeeper out of the window. Kind of skinny, but what the hell. Magaracz turned back to the window and tried to picture Green grappling with the woman, then gave it up and shifted his gaze to the panorama. Another plant closed down last week; another chimney making no more smoke.

"Up here you can watch the smokestacks getting cold all over Trenton," he said.

Green rattled his paper. "They will not warm up again in our lifetime," he rejoined. "Winston Churchill. Or someone like him."

Magaracz grunted, and thought to himself: *Here's a scenario. Green made a smart-ass remark like that, and then Muriel Engelhardt went to throw him out of the window. There was a struggle, and then . . .*

Stan Green went on philosophizing.

He was thinking of death — death in general, but more specifically, death in Trenton.

Here in this city, which some said was itself dying, death was a serious matter, deserving of public notice

43

and public mourning. Upon the death of the great, if anyone in town could be so called, front-page obituaries appeared in the papers, viewings and funerals were held, long lines of cars snaked with their lights on from church or synagogue to some cemetery in the surrounding townships (all the graveyards in Trenton being full long ago). Sometimes you could look down from that window and see them.

And as for the death of the small — well, right here in the paper was an example. Green's *Trentonian* was open to the obituary page. A baby boy was dead, of an address in a run-down part of town. The survivors, as the paper styled them, were the child's teenaged mother, the maternal grandparents and great-grandparents, and a long list of aunts and uncles, all at home, as well as the young father, of a different surname and address. Even this little one's death had surely grieved his family, who had crowned him with the name of Shahjehan, though no doubt they could scarcely afford to feed him. Not a sparrow falls.

Muriel's story was right underneath:

Mrs. Muriel Engelhardt, 51, fell from a window of the New Jersey Division of Mental Rehabilitation Building Friday evening a few minutes after the office had closed for the day. She was pronounced dead at the scene.

Born in Roxbury, Mass., Mrs. Engelhardt was a resident of Boston before moving to Hamilton Township 13 years ago. She was a Senior Clerk Bookkeeper for the Division of Mental Rehabilitation, where she was employed for the past five years.

A member of the Saint Francis Altar Rosary Society,

Mrs. Engelhardt is survived by her sister, Mrs. Armand LaPorte of Boston, a son, Edward Engelhardt Jr., of Denver, Colo., and several nieces and nephews. Burial will be in St. Joseph's Cemetery, West Roxbury, Mass. A memorial Mass will be celebrated at St. Francis Church in Trenton at 9 A.M. Tuesday.

Contributions may be made to the Delaware Valley Suicide Hotline Foundation.

Very discreet, Green thought. Much better than a page one headline proclaiming, "Neurotic Woman Leaps to Death." Much better for the Division, much more considerate of the feelings of Muriel's son. Notwithstanding the arguments of people like Rose Petrowski. Green had overheard her earlier insisting that the boy ought to face up to it, the wickedness of what he had done, abandoning his poor mother and so on.

Green wondered what they would write when his brother Leo died. It would rate a paragraph or two. "Derelict Perishes in Alley. Foul Play Ruled Out.

"An autopsy has revealed that a diseased liver was the cause of the death yesterday of Leo P. Green. Green was a lifelong resident of Trenton," etc.

Perhaps there would be a public outcry. Letters to the editor would appear, some from retired Trentonians in Florida and the Bahamas, deploring the fate of the homeless and old in Trenton.

Would Stan Green still be here to read them? Or, himself in the Bahamas, might he not write letters of his own? Behind his newspaper, where Magaracz could not observe him, Green pulled out his top desk

45

drawer and gazed again at the snapshot he had stolen from Roberta's trip pictures. He thought of Magaracz the other day trying for God knows what reason to tempt Green into confessing a lust for money or fast women. Little did he know.

Do I dream of the Big Score? Certainly not, Green had told him, and even as he uttered the words he saw himself on a plane, headed far away from his tired wife and incredibly selfish daughters, with Roberta in the next seat. Perhaps if he could give her a lot of expensive things.

He looked at the picture, seeing in his mind himself (thin, white, his black trunks baggy) sipping a piña colada, with his arm around the tanned and greasy lovely in place of her husband's arm. Take these diamonds, little sweetheart. Take this caviar.

That he couldn't swim, that he was allergic to the sun and never drank alcohol, for some reason never dimmed the fantasy. All he needed was a lot of money, or for Sheila and the girls to leave him. Or all he needed was an hour alone with Roberta. If I could be with you, for just one hour. Surely the force of his passion would be irresistible.

He thought of the caseworker with the curly beard and chest hair who had come into the office last week. Roberta had responded to him, Stan could tell. Maybe if he changed his style. Maybe if he stopped shaving, left his tie home, opened his shirt to there. Bones and gray wool. Would that impress her?

Angela went on meeting Freddy, in their little home by the elevator works.

46

"Freddy, the women are saying she killed herself out of guilt, because she took those checks."

"Yeah, so what," he said.

"That couldn't be the reason. You know that."

"Well, she was crazy. You know how it is with middle-aged women. They're all washed up, so they kill themselves. It happens all the time."

Suddenly, and for the first time since the day some months ago when she fell in love with Freddy, Angela realized that there was something about his face that suggested a rodent. "It doesn't either happen all the time," she said.

"Well, what do you think, then?" he said.

"I think maybe she knew they were blaming her, and she couldn't stand it, and that's why she killed herself."

"Oh, right," he said. "It's our fault." It was his little teeth, she thought, or else his pointy nose. Something. He didn't understand about women, that was for sure. He didn't know what they went through. She was crying now.

"Aw, shut up, for Christ's sake. Aw, Angie, stop it. Hush. Be quiet. They'll hear us up here."

"I can't help it. She was, like, my mother's age. My mother's too young to die."

"Everybody's too young to die, baby," he said. "They die anyway, okay? That's the way the world is. It has nothing to do with us."

"I wish I was high," she said. "I want to get high."

"I wish I was high, too," he said. "I tell you what. I'll score some reefer for us and we'll get high tonight, okay?"

47

"Okay."

"Now blow your nose and cheer up, and we'll go back to work, okay?"

"Okay, Freddy."

They straightened themselves up, and folded the blanket, and tiptoed down the iron stairs.

Freddy went on abusing state time.

Roberta was out of her office. Unobserved, Freddy crept in and used her phone to call a guy he knew.

The guy pointed out to Freddy that payday was still a week away. "Where are you going to get the bread," the guy said, "if you didn't have it last Monday?"

Freddy had forgotten. He thought a minute, then said, "No problem, man. Now I think of it, I can lay my hands on nine thousand dollars anytime."

The guy expressed surprise, but offered Freddy dope in great variety and quantity.

"No, man, I don't want to deal; I just want to, like, party," said Freddy. "What about the stuff you had last week?"

The guy still had some.

"Well, all *right*," said Freddy. "Save me fifty dollars' worth."

Charlie Delpietro went on looking for the silver lining.

"I feel terrible about Muriel, of course, but at least I guess it solves our case," he said to Magaracz.

"How do you figure?"

"Easy, Nick. Muriel stole the checks, then she jumped out the window in remorse. A damned shame, but at least I'm in the clear. You can stay on until the end of the week if you want." He lit up a cigar.

"Where are the checks, then?" said Magaracz. "The cops couldn't find them in her apartment, which, I might add, seemed to have been torn up before they got there. And who were those two strange guys who turned up in the office?"

"Oh, yeah, them. They didn't look so strange, Nick."

"Then maybe you'd like to tell me who they were."

"Auditors?" Delpietro ventured.

"They told the watchman they were cops. The cops said they didn't send anybody."

"I don't know," Delpietro said. "FBI guys, maybe. Insurance detectives. State cops."

"There's something I think you ought to know. That windowsill has scuff marks all over it that weren't there Friday."

"Nick, what are you trying to say?"

"Something stinks about this case, Charlie. I think you ought to get some security up here, the Capitol Police maybe, or a full-time state cop."

Delpietro took a good puff on his cigar. "You're empire-building, Nick," he said.

"What's that supposed to mean?"

"It's evident. You want to set up a whole crime-fighting empire up here, even after the crime is gone. I understand the impulse, Nick. I've given in to it myself sometimes." Puff.

Magaracz fought down an impulse to lay one across Delpietro's smiling, bearded chops. He considered in-

49

stead the bookkeepers' office, a bunch of nice ladies, menaced by an unknown force, their fate in the hands of this stupid ape cousin of his wife's, this . . . state worker. How to get through to that little pea-brain? What, for instance, would scare him?

Bad publicity.

"Look, Charlie," said Magaracz, trying to sound friendly, "I wouldn't kid you. I think we haven't heard the last of this. I really think those women are in danger. What if something else happens to one of them, and it comes out that there was no security? How's that going to look in the *Star-Ledger*?"

Delpietro put his cigar down and stopped smiling. "That's a point," he said. "You have a point there. I tell you what. Why don't you stay on for two more weeks, just until everything cools down. Nothing's going to happen, I'm sure of it, but in case it does, well, you'll be looking after my girls, right? Just in case you happen to be right. Which I doubt."

But that very day two of the stolen checks were cashed.

6

WHEN THE STOLEN checks came to light it was the following Monday. Rose Petrowski was balancing the monthly bank statement for the Patient Allowance Account. There were neat piles of hand-sorted yellow checks all over her desk. She was matching the numbers and amounts against a computer printout from the bank. Although Mr. Delpietro, the supervising accountant, insisted that the bank's computer always got it right, Eunice Fogarty, the head clerk-bookkeeper, knew better. It was simply another indication of his youth and silliness. So in spite of the misguided instructions of her supervisor, Eunice always had one of her girls go over the checks one by one.

"Geez-oh-man," Rose said softly.

"Something wrong?" said Eunice, from her desk at the front of the room.

"Here's two of those stolen checks. I thought we put a stop on them. They've been cashed."

The adding machines stopped. Eunice's girls were all ears.

Eunice said, "We only put stops on the ones over twenty-five dollars, remember? Mr. Delpietro said it

51

would cost too much otherwise to make it worthwhile."

"Let's see the endorsement on the back," said Ella. "Maybe we'll know the writing."

Eunice stood up. "And what makes you think any of us might know the writing, Ella, may I ask? Don't tell me you believe those stories. I would think, Ella Peterson, that anyone who had worked in this bureau for thirty years, as you have, would know better than to suspect any of my girls of stealing checks."

"I didn't mean anything by it, Eunice," Ella said.

"Or maybe you think poor dead Muriel took them," Eunice went on.

"No, no. I don't think Muriel took them," said Ella, near tears.

"All right, then," said Eunice. "Rose, give me those checks." She took them to her desk, where there was a strong light, and adjusted her bifocals. "They're both signed in the same handwriting, all right, but it's very wavery, as if whoever it was had used his left hand," she announced to the waiting office.

"Who are they made out to?" asked Rose.

Eunice turned the checks over. "Horace Pollack, care of the Boardwalk View Rest Home for the Disturbed Elderly. Philomena Del Vecchio, care of the Boardwalk View. Rose, isn't that the place in Atlantic City that called you last week and threatened to throw all our patients into the street if their checks didn't come?"

"Right," said Rose. "The manager called. He was really nasty. And the money wasn't even supposed to be his. It was for haircuts and stuff for the patients."

"That's right," said Eunice, reading the checks. "Twenty-five dollars and no cents, Patient Allowance."

"What now, Eunice?" said Rose.

Eunice handed her back the checks. "Form MR-thirty-seven-A," she said. "Report of Forgery, in quadruplicate. Staple each copy to a clear copy of the check, front and back. One copy for the file room, one copy to the bank, one copy to the post office, and one copy to the district office in Atlantic City. The one for the D.O. goes with the affidavits. I've got the forms for all the covering letters in my desk. Oh, yes, you'd better make extra copies of everything for Mr. Delpietro. He's very interested in those checks, he says."

"Do you want me to call that guy at the Boardwalk View?"

"No," said Eunice. "If he's as nasty as you say, you'd better not fool around with him. Leave that to the caseworker. Just send the papers to Atlantic City by interoffice mail. The worker will take it to the Boardwalk View to get signed. That's what she gets paid for."

"Right," said Rose.

In his office atop the Boardwalk View Rest Home in Atlantic City, Edward B. Franklin was receiving his sons. They were digging their feet in the shag carpet and imploring him for money.

"I'll try Trenton again," said Franklin. There was a telephone number listed in the state government directory for a supervising accountant of the Mental Rehabilitation Division's Bureau of Fiscal Affairs. Franklin instructed his secretary to call that number and keep calling it until she got the supervising accountant on the line for him.

After some minutes and a certain amount of secretarial fencing between his girl and the supervising accountant's girl, Franklin found himself talking to Charles Delpietro.

"I want to know what happened to the checks that were supposed to come to my facility," Franklin said. "I dined with the Commissioner last night, and he, too, is very interested." This last was a lie, but it was often efficacious.

"Ah, we're right on top of the situation, sir," said Delpietro. "In fact, only this morning two of those stolen checks came back with the bank statement, cashed." There was a rustling of papers. "We think that one of the women here may have taken them, and we expect to recover them shortly. Unfortunately the woman jumped out of our office window the week before last. Out of remorse, some of us thought."

"And she cashed two checks before she killed herself?" said Franklin.

"Well, actually, now that you mention it, I see here that the checks were cashed several days after she died."

"I see," said Franklin.

"So it must have been for some other reason that she . . ."

"Presumably."

Franklin heard a slippery squeak, like the sound of a bureaucrat's sweaty palm losing its grip on the phone. "Tell you what, Mr. Franklin," Delpietro said. "Why don't you come to Trenton? I'm sure my girls in the bookkeeping department will be glad to straighten this whole thing out for you."

"I'll be there this afternoon," said Franklin, and hung up.

He looked up. The boys were staring at their shoes.

"Junior," said Franklin. "Did you two go to Trenton when I told you to?"

"No, Dad."

"What happened there?" said Franklin.

"Nothing."

"Did you throw that woman out the window?"

"Of course not, Dad. What do you think we are?"

"How did she come to go out the window?" Franklin pursued.

"Dad, we don't know, honest," said Junior. "We were just going to, like, ask her some questions, and the next thing we knew, she was out the window."

"We thought she had Junior's checks," said Hanky.

"She was going to leave town," said Junior.

"We thought we could scare her into telling us where they were by hanging her out the window."

"We slipped."

"She fell."

"It was an accident."

"It wasn't our fault."

Franklin looked at his sons in silence for a while. Then he took a pill, washing it down with Scotch from a flask in his desk drawer, and turned to gaze out the window, far away over the ocean.

"What do you want us to do now, Dad?" said Junior.

He turned to face them again. "Don't do anything," he said. "Stay out of Trenton and don't do anything else at all. If you have to stay indoors to keep the loan shark from getting you, then stay indoors. If you like, I can advance you plane fare out of the dietary budget. I'm expecting some checks from Medicare in today's mail. You might leave the state."

"We could go to Vegas," Junior said. "But, no, Big Frank would find us there. Big Frank has a long arm."

"Why don't you go to college?" said his father. "That would never cross Big Frank's mind."

"Dad," Hanky said, "it's April. People don't go to college in April."

"No, I don't suppose so," Franklin said. "Stay indoors, then."

"But, wait a minute," said Junior. "Who was it that cashed the checks? It wasn't that lady. She's dead. Somebody else must have them."

"Never mind," said Franklin. "I'll take care of it. As soon as I get a look at the checks I'll know where they were cashed, and then I can go there and ask around. You two just keep out of sight. And for God's sake, keep out of Trenton."

"All right, Dad," they said.

Franklin could no longer deny it. Something was wrong with his boys. They could not function effectively outside Atlantic City. It was like taking some rare tropical fish out of a protected lagoon in the South

Seas and dumping them in the broad ocean. Either they began to bite everything in sight or they started to die. He sighed. "Just stay indoors."

"Okay, Dad."

Franklin got to Trenton in good time but he had trouble parking the car. At last he found a place for it behind the Commons in the city lot. The Mental Rehabilitation Building was just a short walk away.

"Mr. Franklin!" called a voice, as he passed the steps of the church. To his horror one of the derelicts sprang up and confronted him, blocking his way.

"I saw your boys at the agency the other day."

"What?" Franklin saw now that the man was a former patient at Boardwalk View. Brown? No, Green. Leo Green.

"I saw your boys at the agency, when that woman was killed. They were telling people they were cops. Your boys cops now, Mr. F.?" The old man winked, a burlesque grimace that made the wrinkles extend up his scalp, under his stubbly hair. "I remember them from the time I was at your place. They used to come and see you in the office there. I didn't say anything. How about giving me five?"

For a loathsome moment Franklin thought the old creature meant to shake hands with him. Then he realized he was shaking him down. "Here," said Franklin, handing Leo Green a five-dollar bill.

"Thanks, Mr. F.," he said. "I'll remember you for this. But don't worry; I'll keep my mouth shut." Then the man did actually shake his hand, pawing him on the shoulder and breathing sour wine into his face. "See you again soon."

"Just don't put your hands on me," Franklin muttered, but the old bum was already scurrying away in the direction of the liquor store. "This won't do at all," Franklin thought. He diverted his steps to a nearby fast-food place, there to drink some coffee, take a pill, and think.

The shopping-bag lady who wore two pairs of glasses at once was a former normal person. She had worked as a clerk in Eunice Fogarty's bookkeeping unit before some life crisis pushed her from being a little strange to being completely crazy. She quit her job then, and started wearing funny clothes and painting her face white and red. Eunice would see her sometimes sitting on the steps of the Presbyterian church with her shopping bag, or loping along the Commons with her odd lurching walk, or exchanging abuse with one of the winos.

Even in a town as full of grotesques as Trenton, New Jersey, people stared at Ruth Ann Walker on the street.

First of all, she was nearly six feet tall. Then there were the old black wig, and the makeup, and the two pairs of glasses, and the clothes, bright rags and oddments she found in the trash or at the thrift shop. The effect she created was startling.

And she wasn't shy. She would talk to anybody, and say anything. Sometimes when a good-looking man walked by she would offer him her body in a deep loud voice.

Worst of all, she liked to drop in from time to time on her old office mates.

Ten days after the death of Muriel Engelhardt, Charlie Delpietro still hadn't made up his mind that increased security was needed in the accounting department. So nobody stopped her when Ruth Ann walked into the Mental Rehabilitation Building and took the elevator to the twelfth floor.

"Hi, Eunice," she said in her resonant voice, striking a pose in the bookkeepers' doorway.

"Oh, hello, Ruth Ann," Eunice said with dismay. She tried to catch the eye of Rose Petrowski. Eunice and Rose had fixed it up between them that the next time Ruth Ann showed up in the office one of them would keep her talking and the other would go call the police. That way Ruth Ann would be taken away and put someplace warm and safe, as she was becoming an obvious danger to herself. Last week she had come up to Rose in the Public Library and had said, "I would join this club, but I don't have the money," in a wise voice, and then she had gone away.

Rose looked up from her work and gave a nod. Then she got up and went through the door to Roberta's office, where she could use the phone unobserved.

"What's new, Ruth Ann? What are you doing these days?" Eunice said desperately, wondering how long the police would take getting there.

Ruth Ann grinned horribly, exposing her missing front tooth. "I'm making these hats," she said. "Would you like to buy one?"

"Oh, Ruth Ann — I don't think —" The "hats," as they all knew, were worthless tangles of dirty yarn that Ruth Ann thought she was crocheting. She kept them balled up inside her wig.

"I only want a dollar for them," Ruth Ann said. "I have three colors today, one to match every outfit."

"But I don't really need a hat, dear," said Eunice.

"Will you give me the price of a pack of cigarettes, then? Say, that isn't very much. I would do it for you." Her voice was tragic. "Come on, Eunice. Have a little common humanity."

"All right, I'll buy a hat," said Eunice, feeling somehow defeated.

"What color do you want?" Ruth Ann asked cheerfully.

"Blue," said Eunice. Ruth Ann took her wig off, a horrible sight, and plucked out a snarl of blue yarn.

"Here you are," said Ruth Ann. "Wear it in good health." Something was crawling on it.

Eunice gave her the dollar, and she turned and started out of the room. "Wait, don't go," said Eunice. "I want to — er — visit."

"I have to go to the bathroom," Ruth Ann said. "I'll come right back."

When she was out of sight Eunice clawed madly through her desk drawer for the spray can of insecticide that she had brought in the time they had the ants. Finding it, she sprayed the "hat" until it was no longer moving.

In a minute Ruth Ann was back.

"I couldn't get in," she said. "Old Leo the wino is lying up against the door. Does anybody have a cigarette? I just feel so awful. Somebody pushed me."

60

A few of the women looked up at these strange announcements, but the others knew that anything Ruth Ann said could mean anything, or nothing, and they paid no attention.

"Rose has a cigarette," said Eunice, "don't you, Rose? Did you make the phone call? The one we talked about?"

"I made the call," Rose said, "after Her Highness got off the line. We should have some results quite soon." She handed a cigarette to Ruth Ann, who had plopped herself and her shopping bag down on the wooden chair by Eunice's desk in an attitude of weary dejection.

"You don't care, do you," Ruth Ann accused, "if people push me. You don't even mind if there's blood all over the floor. Fire extinguishers can jump off the wall, and bash people's brains out, so they lie there like broken eggs, and it's all the same to you. Well, just you wait, my girl, until you have to go to the bathroom as bad as I do. Then you'll sing another tune."

"How long?" said Eunice.

"They said five minutes," said Rose.

"He was big and nasty," Ruth Ann raved. "He had bug eyes and his fingers were fat on the ends. He gave me such a push." She rubbed her shoulder. The shopping bag fell to the floor. "You know," she said, brightening, "maybe a couple of you could drag him out of the way so I could get in."

"The bug-eyed man?" Eunice asked politely.

"No, he ran away. Leo. Leo the wino. Didn't I just

tell you he was lying dead outside the ladies' room door, with his brains all over the fire extinguisher? I'm sure it must have jumped off the wall and hit him. Things do that. You know, the sidewalk in front of Miss Daisy's boardinghouse got me that way only last week. I was walking along, minding my own business, and before I knew it there was this sidewalk coming at me. Things turn on you." She looked first at Rose and then at Eunice, gazing sadly over the tops of her two pairs of glasses.

"Ain't it the truth," said Rose.

Eunice said, "Rose, go and see whether our friends are on the way, will you?"

"Could you give me a light first?" Ruth Ann asked.

"Oh, yeah," said Rose. "Sure, sweetie. My gosh, I forgot all about giving you a light."

"What did you think I wanted a cigarette for, unless I was going to light it? You people must think I'm crazy."

Rose gave her a light, but she couldn't help laughing at that, and when she laughed Ruth Ann began to laugh, and then Eunice, and soon the three of them were just laughing and laughing.

Suddenly Ruth Ann stopped. "Oh, dear," she said. She got up, picked up her shopping bag, and began to back toward the door. "Oh, dear. If they find out, I'll have to go back. Maybe they'll shock me again." Eunice and Rose looked at each other, and then at the puddle on the chair.

Someone screamed.

It was Roberta the Secretary, out in the hall. In the

confusion that followed, no one noticed that Ruth Ann kept right on going out the door.

Nick Magaracz got off the elevator and noticed at once that things were not right. Moaning sounds and sobbing were coming from the bookkeepers' office, and there was a strange mound in the hall by the ladies' room door, with a nervous cop standing over it. A paper tablecloth covered the mound, printed with pink and blue bunnies and big letters spelling "Happy Birthday." Feet stuck out from underneath. There were holes in the soles of the shoes. The ankles were thin.

"The ladies wanted to cover him," said the cop in answer to Magaracz's stare. "This was all they had."

7

Eunice fogarty met Magaracz at the door to the bookkeepers' office. "There's been a terrible accident," she said. "It's Stan Green's brother Leo." He glanced again at the heap by the ladies' room door, with the battered shoes protruding.

"What happened?" he said.

"It was the fire extinguisher. Somehow it must have come loose from the wall and hit the poor man on the head." She said it hopefully, but the policeman standing by the body shook his head slowly from side to side. "He's taking it pretty hard," Eunice added.

Magaracz would have said he was taking it pretty well, considering he was dead, but then he realized she meant the brother, Stan Green. There he sat in Eunice's chair in the front of the bookkeepers' office, white as dough, staring. Roberta the Secretary and two of the bookkeepers patted his shaking hands and tried to give him tranquilizers.

"His wife and daughters are away," Eunice murmured. "We don't quite know what to do."

The sobbing sounds were coming from Little Angela, slumped over her desk holding her head.

64

"Is Angela related too?" Magaracz asked.

Eunice said, "No, she's been kind of high-strung lately. We called her mother. You know Deirdre; she works downstairs in Records. She should be here in a minute, if the police let her come up."

Ella, the senior citizen, was arguing with the second policeman, who seemed to be trying to take a statement. She said, "Why? What do you have to know my age for? What's that got to do with anything?"

"Miz Peterson," said the officer, "It's on the form. I have to put it down."

"Well, I don't think it's your business or anybody else's how old I am. What do you think of that? What's more, I haven't committed any crime."

"Look, lady, give me a break," the officer begged. Magaracz backed out the door and went to talk to the policeman who was standing by the body.

"You guys sure got here fast," said Magaracz. "This can't have happened more than five minutes ago. I wasn't gone much longer than that."

"Didn't happen to catch anybody leaving the scene?" the policeman said.

Magaracz thought about it. He had gone down in the elevator, bought a pack of cigarettes, questioned the snack bar lady about the day that Muriel was killed, turned around to go back up. . . . "Nobody but that bag lady with the two pairs of glasses."

"Right," said the policeman. "We came to pick her up. Homicide hasn't even got here yet. We got a call to come and get a crazy woman. When we got here she was gone, and all hell was breaking loose. Those women were all screaming and that guy in the chair was passed out in a dead faint."

"The victim here is his brother," Magaracz offered.

"No kidding. I thought he was just some bum."

The bookkeepers sat at their desks like good children when the men from Homicide arrived with their flash cameras and their soft chalk. Magaracz sat with them. Luckily someone had cleaned off the chair by Eunice's desk, and there he waited, eavesdropping and thinking, for the police to begin taking statements.

The women were too upset to work.

"I tell you, Eunice," said Rose, "any more of this and we'll all be ready to take our shopping bags and go sit on the curb."

"Offer it up, Rose," said Eunice.

"Whatever happened to Ruth Ann, anyway?" said Rose.

"Oh, my heavens!" Eunice said.

"What?"

"All that rant of Ruth Ann's about seeing a man in the hall. You remember, she said he pushed her and then ran away."

"You mean . . ."

"It was probably true all the time. Ruth Ann saw the killer."

She called out to the detective in the hall, but he said to wait; it would only be a little while longer. More men had arrived, bringing a stretcher. They seemed to be taking away the remains.

Stanley Green wandered in from the secretary's office and paced aimlessly among the desks.

"Stan," Eunice said, "I really think we should try to get in touch with your wife. Is she at your house at the shore?"

He stared at her blankly. "There's no phone," he said.

"Shall I call the Sea Isle City police department? I can tell them to notify your family that your brother is dead."

"No, it's okay. . . . She'll call me tonight from a pay phone. I'll tell her then." He sat on her desk and began to hook her paper clips together.

"But, Stanley, Sheila ought to be with you. You shouldn't be alone at a time like this."

"She never liked my brother."

All the more reason to tell her, thought Magaracz. *It might make her day.* For no reason, a picture flashed in his mind, or, to be more exact, a snapshot: Roberta, clad only in her "resort wear," smiling up from Stan Green's desk drawer. Maybe something was going on between them.

What if Stan Green had taken the checks to woo Roberta?

True, nine grand wouldn't go very far with a woman like that, and the two would have made a ridiculous couple. Magaracz tried to picture it: her, tanned, slim, young, vivacious, expensively dressed and cared for, and him, pale, scrawny, middle-aged, mournful, and seedy. But maybe nine thousand was only the tip of the iceberg. Millions of dollars went through this accounting office every month.

And as for a miserable wreck like Green attracting a dish like Roberta, Magaracz had seen stranger things in his time. The tastes of women were not to be understood. Look at the Weasel, for instance. He was a tremendous success with women.

But all this was important only if it led to finding the checks. Industrial espionage. That's what Magaracz was here for. No longer did Nicholas Magaracz make his living by following adulterous couples around.

Still. What if this affair was the actual motive for the crime? Muriel finds out, and out the window with her. Leo finds out, and whango.

When at last the police had finished taking everyone's statement, Magaracz found that there was a little crowd of workers afraid to go home by themselves.

"We're parked in the public parking garage," Eunice said to Magaracz. "Would you mind very much walking us over there? We'll be all right as soon as we get in our cars."

"It's so scary in there after everyone has gone home," said Rose. The other two stragglers were Stan and Roberta, but Stanley was in no shape to play the manly protector.

"And if you could take Stan home," Eunice said. "Or to his doctor's. You don't look at all well, Stanley. I really think you should see a doctor. I only wish your wife were home."

Roberta stepped up and took Stan Green by the hand. "Eunice," she said, "I told you before, I'll take Stan home. I go right past his house, and it's out of Nick's way." She patted Green's hand some more. "Unless you think you should see the doctor, Stan."

They all stood around him in a ring, breathless with concern for his health. Green sat up straighter. The color was beginning to come back to his face. He stood, swaying.

"I'll be fine," he said. "Just so I don't have to stand and wait for a bus."

"Anything I can do?" Magaracz offered.

"Thank you, no," said Green.

"Just come with us to the car," said Rose. "We're all parked on the fourth deck."

The sun was setting behind it when they came out of the great black building. Magaracz looked across at the steps of the church, half hoping to see Ruth Ann, the only eyewitness, but all the bums had gone. There was a chill in the air and the wind was picking up. Hardly anyone was on the street.

The little group walked quickly to the parking deck, glancing over their shoulders from time to time.

Magaracz reflected that he would have to call Charlie Delpietro and tell him about all this. Delpietro had taken the afternoon off, to play golf, Magaracz suspected, and knew nothing of the latest developments. He would call him from his own detective agency office, which was quite nearby, as soon as these people were safely away.

The two cars were parked side-by-side, a silver Corvette and an old blue Plymouth. Carefully they looked inside the Corvette, and then Roberta slithered in, followed by Stanley Green.

"You're sure, now, that you'll be all right," said Eunice.

"Fine," said Green. The engine noise was deep and low, like distant artillery, or the pedal tones of a cathedral organ. They rumbled away, tires squealing.

Then Magaracz looked in the trunk of the Plymouth, and under the back seat. There were no murderers hiding. The ladies thanked him and drove down the ramp.

Magaracz still had a theory working in his mind. He walked back to his office and picked up some candy bars and a thermos of coffee. Then he called Charlie D., got no answer, and then he called Ethel to let her know what was up. Stanley Green's address was in his notebook.

It was a neighborhood of well-kept houses, built in the fifties, their trees beginning to attain some stature. All of the streetlights worked. They were incandescent, and glowed noiseless and golden on the rolling green lawns. An occasional child bicycled home to a late dinner.

Green's lawn, alone of all the neighbors', suffered some dread disease, apparent under the streetlight. Beetles, maybe. In Mercerville they said the beetles were bad this year. The silver Corvette was parked in the driveway.

Magaracz parked his Thunderbird in a shadowy place a few houses away where he could watch Green's front door. He had his candy bars and his coffee. Just like the old days.

In the morning the sound of the Corvette's engine woke him. The sun was barely up; bloody sky in the east. He watched the girl drive away alone.

70

The detective stretched himself. His joints were stiff. Frost lay on the ratty lawn. The leftover coffee was cold in the bottom of his thermos, milk filming the top. With chilled fingers he withdrew his pen and notebook from his breast pocket and crossed out a question mark next to the two names. But what of it?

What of it? Suddenly he saw the truth: he had seduced himself. He had slipped into his role of divorce peeper as into a pair of old slippers. But what did it mean to his case, that these two were making it? Anything or nothing.

This was industrial espionage. A roll in the hay was a roll in the hay, but money was money, and murder was something else again. What if he were on the wrong track? He had been hired to find nine thousand dollars in checks.

Find the checks, he said to himself. Or, find the killer, and you have the checks. Then, find the witness and you have the killer.

For if Stan Green, for whatever reason, had offed his brother, Ruth Ann Walker had all but seen him do it. She had seen the killer run away.

Magaracz felt his face, bristly with stubble. The time had come to go after his witness.

8

"AGNES, I'M ALMOST certain that the third bum from the left on the church steps over there — don't look now — is that new Mr. McGratz from Accounting."

The women goggled at the derelicts lined up in the afternoon sun. "Oh, Ella, it couldn't be."

But in fact it was. Magaracz, wearing old clothes and two days' stubble, gripping his bottle of Night Train wine in its paper bag, was communing with the locals.

While outside auditors were combing the Division's books at Magaracz's suggestion, searching for something on Stan Green, the detective himself had gone underground.

"Ruth Ann who?" one of the bums was saying to him.

"Walker. You remember the lady. She was tall, and wore two pairs of glasses and a black wig," Magaracz prompted.

"Black wig. Was she white?"

"Yeah. White. Tall. Walked funny," Magaracz said, thinking that maybe to them her walk wasn't funny. They all had weird walks.

"She owe you money, or what?"

"I owe her money, the truth is," Magaracz said. "She's my cousin. I came into some dough and I thought maybe I'd help her out."

"That's okay," the old bum said. "You can give it to me. I'll give it to her." He began to guffaw and wheeze. Magaracz passed him the bottle of Night Train.

"Why, thank you, brother," the man said after a long pull on it. He wiped his mouth and nose on the ragged sleeve of his coat. "Ruth Ann Walker. Yeah, I remember her."

"Well," said Magaracz, "do you know where I can find her?"

"She hasn't been around for a couple of days. Maybe she's dead." He took a couple of good swallows and passed the bottle back to Magaracz, who pretended to drink from it.

"Where does she live?" Magaracz asked.

The old man gazed at him expectantly. Magaracz handed him the bottle, saying, "Keep it, friend."

"Sometimes she stays at Miss Daisy's."

"Where's that?"

"Miss Daisy's boardinghouse up Greenwood Avenue," the old man said. "Surprised you never heard of it. A lot of us go there sometimes." He told Magaracz the address.

"Much obliged to you, brother," said Magaracz, getting up and shuffling away.

There were doilies on the arms and backs of the maroon plush chairs in Miss Daisy's parlor. There were holy pictures in gilt frames. Bundles of dried plants were tacked over the doorways. Miss Daisy was a black woman, not young, but vital and somehow imposing. She saw that Magaracz was eyeing her dried plants.

"Those herbs keep evil from my house," she said. "Say, are you with the city? You know, I told you people last time I don't own this place anymore. I'm only the manager. The Boardwalk View Corporation bought me out last year when I was having so much trouble."

"Trouble," said Magaracz.

"Trouble with the city," she said. "Regulations. Won't you sit down? You will recall that the sprinkler system and the enclosed stairways cost more than what I was able to raise at the time. Although I told you then, the same as I'm telling you now, that I don't need any nursing home license. All my boarders can take care of themselves. All of them walk, all of them go to the bathroom themselves, they're perfectly competent. You can see that for yourself."

A wan face appeared at the parlor door, leered insanely, and went away. "So you're no longer the owner," said Magaracz.

"No," she said, "but Boardwalk View lets me stay on as manager. With help from Mr. Franklin, of course. He's a real accountant and I must say he's making the place pay."

"Franklin," said Magaracz. "Is he here?"

"No," Miss Daisy said, "he only comes in once a month to go over the books. If you want him you'll find him at their main office in Atlantic City."

"The fact is," said Magaracz, "I'm not with the City of Trenton. I came here to find a woman. They said she might be one of your boarders."

"Well, if she is, she's perfectly happy. All our boarders are perfectly happy here. We take good care of them."

"Her name is Ruth Ann Walker."

Miss Daisy lit a cigarette. "Ruth Ann Walker. That poor girl. Do you know she used to have money? Took it all out of the bank and gave it away. Now she begs for cigarettes. That girl is in bad shape."

"No kidding? Where is she now?" said Magaracz.

"Ruth Ann left yesterday. Came home in the middle of the afternoon, changed her clothes, and packed her things all up, what there was of them. Said she didn't like the climate here anymore, and she was going where she could warm up. Said she was taking the train to Atlantic City."

"Do you think she could get along by herself there? Where would she go?" Magaracz asked.

"I'm not sure she could even get there at all, if she was going by train," said Miss Daisy. "You have to take the bus. Trains don't go there."

"Does she know anybody down there? Anybody she might visit? Anyplace she might go?"

"She might go straight to the Boardwalk View, with her Social Security and all. That'd be her idea of a vacation. You know, they have color television. I don't think she knows anybody to stay with. And that girl is too crazy to be going around by herself in a town where they want to make a nice impression on the tourists."

75

"What do you think would happen?"

She puffed on the cigarette. "Cops would pick her up. Put her away in a place like Ancora."

It was an idea. Magaracz thanked her and went home to tell Ethel he would have to be taking another field trip.

The Boardwalk View Rest Home for the Disturbed Elderly was a magnificent piece of decayed Victoriana, a four-story wedding cake with a tower, nibbled by rats. In the gay nineties it was a fashionable watering place. Now it was a home for old crazies on public assistance.

Sharon Saperstein approached the Boardwalk View without thinking about its architectural or historic significance. She was used to unpleasant places, and paused while getting out of her official State of New Jersey car only long enough to be sure that no one was waiting in the parking lot to jump on her.

Five years a caseworker, two years in possession of her Master of Social Work degree from Rutgers, Ms. Saperstein was just short of the condition known to her fellows as "burnout," a state somewhere between despair and apathy in which all one's clients begin to look alike. She was waiting for her promotion to casework supervisor. In this position she would be insulated from the griefs of her unhappy clients by ten caseworkers and a thick layer of paperwork. If the promotion did not come through this year she meant to quit and become a waitress.

Boardwalk View was not too bad as these places

went. The smell of urine and feces, while noticeable, was not absolutely overpowering, and was mitigated somewhat by the smell of disinfectant. In spite of the old-fashioned exterior of the building Ms. Saperstein could see that she was in a modern facility by such fashionable details as the Reality Board, posted prominently between the pharmacy closet and the nurse's station. It proclaimed:

Today is:	Wednesday, April 8
The Weather is:	Cloudy
The Next Meal is:	LUNCH
The Next Holiday is:	Good Friday

It was felt that the posting of this information would help the patients to experience reality.

There was a small young woman in a white uniform at the desk, who looked up with eyes all ringed with dark green pencil and asked Ms. Saperstein if she could help her.

"I've come to see Mr. Pollack and Mrs. Del Vecchio," said Ms. Saperstein.

"Oh, yes, you would be the worker with the checks," the attendant said. "Mr. Franklin said he wanted to see you right away when you got here."

"Mr. Franklin?"

"Our business manager. I thought you knew him. He wanted to look at the canceled checks, I believe he said." She pressed a button behind the counter.

"No, I've never been here before," the caseworker said. "I took over this case from Miss Garcia."

"Mr. Franklin particularly wants to see you."

77

"But I'd really like to see Mr. Pollack and Mrs. Del Vecchio first," Ms. Saperstein said. "It was their signatures that were forged to these checks and I need for them to examine the signatures and sign these affidavits. Will they be in the dayroom?"

"Mr. Franklin will be right with you."

A little elevator door opened across the hall, and a man came out. He was sleek and manicured and expensively tailored, but despite his prosperous appearance his upper lip was bedewed with sweat, and his hands with their oddly shaped fingertips trembled slightly. Ms. Saperstein wondered, without really caring, whether Mr. Franklin ever dipped into the pharmacy closet.

"Hold my calls," he said to the attendant. He took Ms. Saperstein's elbow in his clammy hand and steered her into the elevator, which climbed five floors to his office.

"Sharon Saperstein, Mr. Franklin," she said, as they clanked upward. "I brought some things for Mr. Pollack and Mrs. Del Vecchio to look over and sign. Since I already have your signature on the Affidavit of Lost or Stolen Check, in connection with the other checks that were missing, I really didn't think it was necessary to disturb you."

"No trouble," he said. "I want to see those checks that were cashed." There was Binaca on his breath.

"Mr. Franklin, those checks would be for Mr. Pollack and Mrs. Del Vecchio to see," she said, feeling more and more ill at ease. "In any case they aren't the checks themselves, but copies." They stepped out into a pale billowy shag rug. Mr. Franklin's desk was a free-form slab of black walnut with two phones, a desk blotter, and a pencil cup on it. There were two nice filing cabinets and a small copying machine. Ms. Saperstein could see the ocean from one of the windows.

"Mr. Pollack is not mentally competent," said Mr. Franklin, as he went through one of the file drawers. It had opened smoothly, silently. "Hardly anyone here is. Mrs. Del Vecchio is too ill to see visitors. But you see, Sharon — may I call you Sharon, by the way?"

"We prefer to use last names, Mr. Franklin, if it's all the same to you."

"Yes. Well, you see —" he drew two notarized papers out of a brown folder —"I have samples of their signatures here. We can compare them."

"Oh, yes, that would be good," said the caseworker, producing her copies of the checks. Mr. Franklin took them from her and held them under the light of his desk lamp. The signatures on the checks were nothing like those on the notarized forms.

"Nice," he said. "You say these checks were taken from your Trenton office at the same time as the others."

She said, "Yes, but —"

"As far as you know, by the same person or persons." He placed them in the copying machine.

"I really couldn't say, Mr. Franklin. Law enforcement isn't my line. I came to get these people's signatures on some affidavits."

He checked the quality of his copy, grunted with

satisfaction, and made another. Then he did the copies of the backs. "We'll need these for our records," he said. He gave her the Division's copies back. His own were very sharp and clear.

Mr. Pollack was in the east dayroom, sitting in front of the television in a wheelchair, along with fifteen or twenty other old people. If he had teeth, he wasn't wearing them. On the screen of the big color TV two women in the costumes and surroundings of the upper middle class were conversing.

"Nancy, I hardly know what to think about Millicent's behavior," said one.

"But, Gloria . . . You mean you haven't heard?"

"What?"

"Millicent told Rod."

A tight closeup appeared of the first woman, drawing in her breath as if to reply. Then two other women appeared, talking in animated tones about laundry detergent. It was all the same to the old people watching the TV, sitting like eggs in an egg box.

"Mr. Pollack?"

"Here," he said, turning his chair a little.

"I'm Sharon Saperstein from the Division of Mental Rehabilitation. I'm taking care of your case now."

"Where's that nice Miss Garcia?"

"Miss Garcia isn't with the Division any more. Mr. Pollack, I'm here about the theft of your monthly allowance check."

"What monthly allowance check?"

"The twenty-five dollars spending money you receive every month in addition to the fees the State pays the Boardwalk View."

"First I've heard of it," the old man said.

"Now, Mr. Pollack, it's a monthly allotment. You get it every month to take care of incidentals."

"Your ass."

Ms. Saperstein decided to try another approach. She showed him the copy of the check. "Is this your signature?"

"No."

"Will you sign this affidavit to that effect?"

"Sure, why not." He signed it. "Say, do you have a cigarette?"

"I'm afraid I don't smoke, Mr. Pollack," she said as she affixed her notary seal.

"Too bad," he sighed. "Miss Garcia smoked. She used to give me a whole pack."

"I wonder when I can see Mrs. Del Vecchio," Ms. Saperstein murmured.

"She's dead," Mr. Pollack said.

"Surely you mean she's very sick and can't leave her room."

"She's been dead and gone for six months. I know dead when I see it, I hope. Didn't the fellows from the Medical College come and take away her body?"

"Mr. Pollack, if that were the case the Division would have been notified and her support checks stopped," said Ms. Saperstein reprovingly.

"Eff you, then, Ms. Bureaucrat, think what you like."

Ms. Saperstein thought, *Senile paranoia.*

81

The others began shushing them. The principals in the TV drama had returned to the screen and were wondering how Brad would take the bad news.

"Well, good-bye, Mr. Pollack," said Ms. Saperstein. "Thank you."

Mr. Pollack grunted.

"He peed on the radiator last week," one of the old women remarked to Ms. Saperstein as she left.

In his tower office, Franklin had read on the check copy the name of the bank and branch where it had been cashed.

It was time for him to go back to Trenton.

9

The Next Meal is: DINNER.

In the kitchen of the Boardwalk View this meal is being prepared. Outside, night is falling. The cavernous kitchen is lit by a single fluorescent light, and by the blinking sign of the Aces 'n' Eights Motor Hotel filtering through a greasy window.

Tonight's dinner will not be a hot meal. The stoves are not lit. The cook, an old man in a stained apron, is dealing bologna like cards onto a seemingly endless row of slices of bread. He is assisted by his grandson, a snuffly child of six or seven, who follows behind him with a jar of mustard, dabbing it on.

A large yellow cat follows after them, walking along on top of the table. The cat puts his feet carefully on the sandwiches, knowing from experience that to step in the mustard is unpleasant. He licks and bites the meat from time to time. As the old man comes around again to put slices of bread on top, the cat sits down on a sandwich, curls his tail around his feet, and begins to groom his fur.

All this is observed by Magaracz as he hides behind the refrigerator. Roaches run over his shoes. He curses himself for having taken the wrong approach.

If only I had told them I was an inspector, he thinks. *Then they would have had to give me a complete tour of the place, right in broad daylight.* Somewhere in there, he believes, lies Ruth Ann Walker the murder witness, maybe drugged, maybe dead, victim of a complicated conspiracy involving corruption in high places. If you could call the civil service title of senior accountant a high place.

But Magaracz was on the case. That afternoon he had thought to find his witness by walking in the front door and asking for her. He failed. It seemed that he antagonized the receptionist.

The Reality Board by the reception area said, "Today is: Friday" when Magaracz stepped up to the counter. He was reasonably sure it was still Thursday, but he checked his watch to make certain. "Excuse me, miss," he said to the young woman behind the counter, "but I think your board is out of whack."

She looked up sullenly and asked whether she could help him.

"I'm looking for a Ruth Ann Walker," he said. "I was told that she was staying here."

"We have no one by that name here," said the girl, returning to her paperwork.

"How can you tell?" Magaracz persisted. "You must have a thousand patients in this place. Do you know them all by name?"

"We have three hundred and seventy-five patients here, and yes, of course I know them all by name." She filed a card she had been filling out and started another one.

Magaracz leaned over the counter, fixed the girl

84

with a level gaze and pushed a business card toward her. The card bore Magaracz's phone number and a fancy false Anglo-Saxon name.

"Miss," he said, "I'm here on behalf of the Eastern-Albatross Insurance Company on an extremely confidential matter. I would appreciate it very much if you would check your files."

With evident disgust she pulled out a drawer of cards. "Walker," she said, poking through them. "I'm sorry, but as I told you before, there is no Ruth Ann Walker in our current patient file."

Magaracz, in the meantime, was gazing all around to see what he could see. He read all the papers on the desk that were visible, since reading upside-down was one of his skills, and then he began to eye the doors and speculate on where they led. The large double doors at the far end of the room were opening.

"Perhaps she's registered under another name," Magaracz offered.

"Sir," said the girl, banging a pencil down on the counter, "all of our patients have to have Social Security numbers before they are admitted. Our patients are receiving federal assistance in most cases. In any event, Boardwalk View has to be prepared to provide if long-term care becomes necessary. We're very careful."

A stretcher appeared in the double doorway, feet sticking up on it, two young men in workmen's clothing wheeling it along.

"I see," said Magaracz. "Hang onto them until you can rake in the pensions."

"I beg your pardon?" the girl said.

"I said I'm sure that correct identification is important under those circumstances." The two men were bringing the stretcher up to the desk.

"Very important," the girl said. "So I'm sure you can see that a case of mistaken identity would be impossible. Now, if you'll excuse me."

"Just the same," said Magaracz, "let me describe this woman to you, and then you can tell me whether you have seen anyone come in here recently who answers this description." He took out his notebook and began to read. Waves of cold were coming from the sheet-covered body on the stretcher, which the two men had wheeled nearly to his elbow.

"White female," read Magaracz. "Five feet, eleven inches tall. That's about my height." Wordlessly the girl handed one of them a form headed "Transfer of Cadaver." The man began to fill it out.

"Mole on left side of nose," Magaracz went on. He was thinking that this description might fit a number of women. The fact was that if you took away the face paint, the strange clothes, and the frowzy wig, what was left? Just another tall, stupendously ugly woman who walked funny.

The telephone rang.

"Boardwalk View Rest Home," the girl said. "No, I'm afraid Mr. Franklin is out for the day. No, I'm very sorry, but he really is out."

The presence of the stiff on the stretcher was working on Magaracz's nerves. How easy it would be for these people to dispose of a dead witness. But, why should they do that? Well, suppose Stanley Green, with his embezzled millions (which through some oversight the state auditors had been unable to find), suppose Stanley Green had paid them to.

Green must have had some dealings with the place when his brother was here. Suppose he slipped them a couple of grand to eliminate a big-mouthed bag lady. They might take it. This crowd wasn't in business for their health. If they were in business for anybody's.

Magaracz lifted the sheet and stared into the dead face. It was not that of Ruth Ann Walker.

"Cute, ain't he?" said one of the men. Shrugging, Magaracz put the sheet back. The girl was telling someone that Mr. Franklin would be sure to call as soon as he came in.

"Yes, sir," she said, as she wrote on a pink pad marked "While You Were Out." "Tolerate . . . no further . . . delay in . . . payment. Yes, I have the message and I'll make sure he gets it." She held the phone away from her ear, frowned at it, and hung it up. "Did the school give you our check they were supposed to give us?" she said to the man who filled out the cadaver form.

"They said to tell you it would be in the mail," he said. He signed the form and gave it to her.

She put it in the "In" basket. "Well, okay, then," she said. "See you next time."

"Till next time," they said, and rolled the body out.

The girl returned to her paperwork. Magaracz coughed, cleared his throat, and hung a little farther over the counter.

The girl looked up at him coldly.

"Do you think you might remember this woman? She would have been wearing funny clothes and a black wig."

"You said her name was what?"

"Ruth Ann Walker."

Something that might have been recognition showed on her face for a second. Then, "No," she said.

"Do you suppose I could have a look around?"

"Certainly not," she said. "Nobody tours the facility except with the permission of Mr. Franklin, and he has gone to Trenton for the day. We don't expect him back for some hours."

"Too bad," Magaracz said. "There's a great deal of money coming to Miss Walker when we locate her. I wish you would mention this to Mr. Franklin, and give him my card, when he comes in."

She answered not a word, but went back to her card-filing.

When she comes off duty, Magaracz thought to himself, *I can come back and search the place.* But he had left his fake health inspector credentials back in Trenton, and was forced to sneak into the kitchen like a common thief. Now he crouched behind the refrigerator, waiting his chance.

At long last upward of three hundred bologna sandwiches and glasses of tepid tea were loaded onto a cart. The old man and the child trundled it out, leaving Magaracz alone with the yellow cat.

Magaracz came out of concealment, weighing alternatives as the cat sniffed his cuffs. There was a fire alarm switch by the stove. To pull it would perhaps be to clear out the nursing home, making a search simple. Yet, how could he bring himself to disturb the poor old patients at their dinner? Much better to put on a white coat, and stroll through the place as if he had every right to be there.

A brief search turned up a suitable lab coat, hanging in the pantry on a rusty nail. The fit was only a little tight.

Up in the tower, in the office of Edward Burkhaus Franklin himself, the nursing home kingpin's sons were searching his desk.

"I know it must be here somewhere," Junior said. "He always unloads his stuff here when he gets back from the field. He writes everything on it."

"Are you sure he got back from Trenton already?" said Hanky, looking under the blotter and dumping over the pencil cup.

"Yeah, I'm sure," said Junior. "Quit making a mess or he'll know we've been in here. He told me he was going this morning to check with that bank and find out what sort of person cashed the checks there. Gertrude told me he stopped at the reception desk an hour ago. He has to have been there and back."

"Is this it?" said Hanky, holding up a pocket notebook.

"Yeah," said Junior, snatching it roughly. "Let's see what's the last thing he wrote in it. 'First Merchant's Bank of Mercer County.' This must be the teller's name. 'Man in early . . .' twenties, I think it says . . . 'tall, fair-haired, face like weasel.'"

"That *guy*," said Hanky. "The mail boy, remember? The hotshot with the fancy van."

"His name . . ."

"Grover?"

"Gruver. With a *u*. Eddie, Freddy . . . Let me see that Trenton phone book." Junior looked up the Weasel's address. "I know that place; it's a big apartment complex outside Princeton. I used to date a girl from there. Let's go; I can find it easy."

"But Dad told us not to leave the building," Hanky said. "Especially he said don't go to Trenton."

"Hanky, I'm not going to spend another day hiding in my damn room when I could pay off Big Frank and be out partying. Come on. We'll pick up some stuff first. We don't want to make any mistakes this time."

They were going down in the elevator as Magaracz was coming up the stairs.

Afterward when Magaracz remembered his stealthy search of the Boardwalk View Rest Home for the Disturbed Elderly only a few things stood out. He remembered the jars of teeth. He remembered the gauze-wrapped tongue depressor dangling from an old person's bed on the end of a string. What was it for? Sometimes he still wondered. It teased his imagination, like the sign that he used to see in the window of the porn store in downtown Trenton: "Booksmags!" What was a Booksmag? What did you do with one?

What use could anyone have for a tongue depressor wrapped in gauze and hanging from a string?

He remembered the thrills — hearing just in time the squeak of the night attendant's crepe-soled shoes, ducking out onto the balcony at the last possible instant to avoid discovery, putting his foot through the rotted decking, saving himself by the tips of his fingers from plunging three stories into the parking lot of the Aces 'n' Eights Motor Inn.

He remembered being surprised to discover that the entire fourth floor was used for living quarters by the proprietor. Pretty comfortably, too, it appeared to Magaracz, as he cast his flashlight beam around the dark apartment from one expensive luxury to another. Class. Real paintings on the wall. Real silver. Rugs that came up to your ankles. On this floor, the plaster wasn't water-damaged, causing Magaracz to ask himself, where did the water come from that stained the lower floors? *Plumbing?* he thought. There was a sound. The elevator had come to the fourth floor and stopped. The door opened.

Luckily Magaracz found room and time enough to hide behind the sofa.

"Hanky?" a voice called out. The lights came on. "Hanky? Junior? Boys?"

Still calling, the newcomer went from room to room and back again. Rummaging noises. Sounds of a drink being poured. "Maybe it's all right," said the voice to himself. The man sat on the sofa, and sighed, and drank. After a very long time he said, "Maybe they're at the casino." Then he got up and left.

Magaracz came out and continued his search of the apartment. Apparently it was occupied by one middle-aged rich man and his two large untidy sons. No bag ladies.

He went up to the tower. There he found only the office of one E. B. Franklin. His business machines. His desk. His files. There, if only he had known how to look for it, Magaracz could have found the evidence of enough wrongdoing to put Franklin away for decades. Yet even if he knew, Magaracz would not have been interested. He was here for only one thing: to find Ruth Ann Walker.

At last he had to admit it to himself. She was not here. Probably she had never been here.

He took the elevator down, left his lab coat on the counter in the deserted lobby, and let himself out. No one saw him.

He had felt so sure that she was there. Now there were no leads. He got into his car, pushing aside the pile of tape cassettes that Charlie D. had given him that morning. Maybe there were clues on the tapes. Maybe Stan Green and Roberta Schwartz had betrayed themselves to his secret microphone. Should he listen to them now?

No. It was time to play blackjack.

The neon sign for the Royal Cosmic Casino was a green planet with yellow rings around it, surmounted by a crown. Magaracz went in and played blackjack until he had lost fifty dollars. Then he headed for the bar.

It was dark. The waitress wore a strange small costume that caused her breasts to sit out like oranges on saucers. Magaracz ordered an old-fashioned. Through the archway at the end of the bar the sounds of the casino floated like something from another world, as did occasional couples, enfolded in clouds of perfume and strong drink.

A young girl came through the archway by herself and sat at the end of the bar. She wore heavy makeup, a tight red dress, and sandals with heels so high she could scarcely walk. Her hair was like angel hair, all yellow curls. There was something familiar about her.

A well-dressed, graying businessman detached himself from the other end of the bar and sat next to her.

"Excuse me, young lady," he said. "I couldn't help noticing that you were alone. I wonder whether you would do me the honor of allowing me to buy you a drink."

Without looking up, the girl said, "Stick it sideways."

The man recoiled, and with the icy dignity of the very drunk, he stalked to Magaracz's booth and sat down opposite him.

One of the other patrons fed the jukebox, causing disco music to boom and howl. Magaracz lit up a cigarette.

Then, through the archway, on wings of song, as it were, humming along with the jukebox, discoed the tall, lithe, unmistakable form of Freddy the Weasel.

He addressed the young woman at the end of the bar. "Hey, baby," he said. "The night is young. Let's dance."

"Go to hell, Freddy," she said.

"No, come on. I want to boogie." He did a few steps around her, embraced her shoulders, and tickled her under the chin.

She said, "Fuck off, you stinking shit."

"Now, sweetie, don't be angry. There's plenty more where that came from."

"That was my entire pay! Two weeks' pay! How could you sit there and gamble away all our money?" She turned her face toward him and Magaracz saw that it was Little Angela from the office.

She didn't seem to recognize Magaracz; it might be that she was consumed with rage and sorrow, and unable to take in any of her surroundings. What would her mother have said, to see her in that outfit? Black mascara was running down under her eyes.

"All our money!" she raved. "I don't even know how you're going to get the van out of the parking lot! And to think — Oh, God! It just makes me want to throw up!"

"Hey," said Freddy. "Come on. I know the parking lot guy. He'll let us have the van back. Me and him are buddies." He had her off the stool, and was leading her gently toward the casino entrance. She shook her head from side to side. "Come and dance," he said. "We're here to have fun. I want to dance with my sweetie." Her recriminations were swallowed by the jangle and clunk of slot machines, and the chants of dealers.

"Would you take it amiss, then, sir, if I were to buy you a drink?" said the rejected businessman.

"Not at all," said Magaracz politely.

"First of all, allow me to introduce myself. I am Edward B. Franklin, Senior," the man said, giving Magaracz his card, which was unreadable in the darkness.

"Pleased to meet you. I'm Nick Magaracz."

"Do you have children, Mr. Magaracz?" the man asked.

"I have a daughter," said Magaracz, "and I want to tell you, I hope I never see the day when she goes to bars dressed like that one." He gestured with his hand toward the departed Angela.

"I have sons," said Franklin. This was followed by a long silence, during which another round of drinks came. Even in the dim light Magaracz could see that the other man looked ill; his face was white and sweat gleamed on his upper lip. He took his drink, apparently a shot of vodka, and downed it. Magaracz noticed the unusual shape of his hands and fingers.

"Family is all that's important in this world, sir," the man went on. "Family is what keeps this country together."

"That's right, brother. No truer words were ever spoken," said Magaracz, thinking of the business that used to come his way when the legislature had respected that institution.

"My sons are not always everything that I want them to be."

"Don't worry about it too much," Magaracz said. "It's a common complaint nowadays. These are rough times to be a parent." He raised his glass. "Happy days."

Franklin held up one finger with its fan-shaped nail, and the waitress brought him another drink. "Your health," he said to Magaracz. "But you see, the younger generation. This —" he gestured in a half-circle with his glass, indicating the darkness, the sleaziness, the gamblers and hopeless people — "this is a growing city. Atlantic City holds out a great future to its young. Excuse me." He took a pill.

"But the young —" He swallowed, with a certain amount of difficulty. "The young must be worthy. They must be ready to make the most of the opportunities that come their way. They must build on the legacy of the past, and not . . . not . . . waste it."

Sounds like he's talking to a high school graduation, Magaracz thought. He said, "I'm sure your boys will be okay." Franklin. Jeez. This was the nursing home guy. Magaracz felt shame. Only an hour ago he had been tossing this guy's apartment. He offered the man a comforting platitude. "Kids today are wild," he said, "but so were we, right? They grow out of it."

"If only that were true," said Franklin.

"It is. You'll see."

"To found a dynasty. That was my aim when I came here, Mr. . . . er . . ."

"Magaracz."

"But my sons, Mr. Magaracz, have been something of a disappointment to me. Nevertheless, I must do what I can for them. We must hope in our children. For if we don't have them, we have nothing. They are our future."

But Magaracz suspected that the future was where

96

you came across it, sometimes with your children and sometimes in a car crash, or maybe at the bottom of the sea, and you came across it soon enough. "Where are your sons now?" he asked politely, realizing too late that it wasn't a good question, from the color of Franklin's face.

"My sons," he mumbled. "It's ten o'clock. Do you know where your children are? I told my sons to stay home. They disobeyed me."

10

FRANKLIN'S BOYS were in Freddy the Weasel Gruver's apartment.

Hanky was prowling like a monkey through Freddy's possessions, playing with everything, almost fainting with covetousness. Freddy had given a great deal of attention to his apartment. Here the bachelor life was lived.

There was, of course, an immense sound system, and a collection of records and tapes containing all the greatest rock and disco hits of the last fifteen years. There was a well-stocked bar, with many liquors and mixers. There was a large puffy thing covered with imitation gorilla hair that Freddy's furniture salesman had called a lounge.

There was a big-screen projector TV, and much video recording equipment. There was a shelf full of homemade videotapes. When Hanky played them they seemed to be views of naked women, young state workers by the look of their hair and makeup, wiggling around on the lounge, and sometimes doing interesting things with Freddy.

There was a bookcase. It held, besides the videotapes, several lurid paperback bestsellers, and eight linear feet each of *Penthouse*, *High Times*, and *Stereo Review*.

There was a balcony with a sliding door, through which the Franklin brothers had gained entrance. It was piled invitingly with brightly colored (if somewhat moldy) pillows, and festooned with twenty-five potted plants in varying stages of ill health. One of them was marijuana. Beyond the balcony there was nothing but woods. Freddy's apartment was in the last building of the complex.

In the bathroom, there were towels on the floor, and used socks, and a few swift cockroaches. Three pairs of men's multicolored nylon briefs hung on the towel rack. Toilet preparations of various kinds cluttered the available flat surfaces. The shower curtain was of clear plastic with flowers on it. A woman had given it to Freddy some time ago but had not stayed to maintain it, so mildew was growing on the hem. Freddy's morning whiskers were still in the sink. The medicine cabinet was crammed with vitamins, cold remedies, prophylactics, and K-Y Jelly.

Hanky closed the cabinet door and groomed his moustache in the mirror, imagining himself the lord of this domain. All those women. Jesus. His father had no idea how to live.

In the bedroom there was a four-posted waterbed and a closetful of disco clothes. Hanky tried a couple of the suits on, but they hung on him. Almost as an afterthought, he tied four ropes to the bedposts to prepare for the business of the evening, for he and his brother had been unable to find the missing checks by searching the apartment.

Then Hanky took the video recorder camera to the kitchen and began to photograph his brother Junior in the act of clipping his nails. The tumbler of Sambuca Romana that Junior had poured himself was empty now, Hanky saw, and he told himself it was time to start watching out. "Hey, Junior," he said, staying out of arm's reach, "how come we don't have stuff like this?"

"I could get an apartment like this anytime I want. Only I got, like, investments to maintain." Clip, clip. "I need to preserve my cash flow." He started to work on his cuticles.

"Oh, yeah, I forgot. You hafta pay off Big Frank."

"Shut up."

"You know, you ought to quit gambling."

"Up your ass, Hanky," said Junior, with a vicious jab at his brother with the point of the nail clippers.

Getting ugly, all right, thought Hanky, and continued to rummage, in the refrigerator now.

"Look at this. It's frozen strawberry daiquiri mix."

"Why don't you make yourself a drink?"

"Yeah, right," said Hanky. "What do you do, stick it in the blender?"

"Yeah, with rum or something."

"Won't it make noise?"

"Right, it will make noise. The neighbors will hear it. Scratch that. Any beer in there?"

"Heineken."

"Good," said Junior. "Open me one."

"When do you think he'll get here?"

"Should be pretty soon," said Junior. "Everything all set up?"

"Yeah," said Hanky, "the ropes and the splinters and the gag." He took a good swallow of beer. "But I can't reach the bed with the chain saw you brought. The cord ain't long enough."

Junior stood up. "Doesn't this dumb ass have an extension cord?" he said.

"There was one," Hanky said, shrugging, "but it wasn't for three prongs."

"Maybe we can fix it. Meanwhile, you go look under the sink in the bathroom, and in the closet. You'd think with all the stuff this guy has lying around . . ."

"Okay, Junior."

"Which reminds me, when he comes in we turn the stereo up real loud, right? That way if he yells or anything before we get the gag on him the neighbors won't hear."

"Right," said Hanky.

Homeward bound on the Atlantic City Expressway, Magaracz listened to tapes.

Charlie D. had argued a long time before he would let Magaracz bug Roberta Schwartz's office. He was willing to call in the auditors to go over Green's books, but not to spy on his own secretary. At last Magaracz simply walked into his office, carrying a large spider plant in a hanging pot, and deposited it on Delpietro's desk.

"What's this for, Nick?"

"This is my sick plant. I brought it from home so I could hang it in Roberta's office where it would get some sun."

"Now look, Nick," said Charlie D.

"Look, Charlie, don't give me any static. I sat up half the night putting this thing together. It'll pick up a whisper at ten yards, and I want it hanging in her office."

"There's no reason for it, Nick."

"No? That little sweetie is up to her neck in this, is the reason. Look, do you want me to solve this case or not? It's beginning to look like you don't. Not only that, I'm beginning to wonder why."

Charlie D. sighed. "All right, Nick," he said, "but you're all wrong about Roberta. She's a good kid."

"Do you know she's boffing Green?"

"I don't believe that for a minute, Nick," said Charlie D.

"Believe it or not. What's more, I think Stan Green killed his brother."

"Come on, Nick. Get serious."

"Did you know there were twenty-three murders in the city of Trenton last year, and seven of them were cases of guys killing their brothers? Ethel's brother the cop told me that."

"So what?" said Delpietro.

"So you have to figure the odds, Charlie."

"Nick, I've known Stan Green for years. He couldn't kill a fly. In fact, I saw him once when he was literally unable to kill a cockroach. He kept hitting on either side of it until it got away. All the women were screaming."

102

"Maybe he thought he was doing his brother a favor," said Magaracz. "Maybe it was euthanasia."

"Youth in Asia? You mean like Bruce Lee?"

"Mercy killing. Suppose your brother was a bum on the streets. Don't you think he'd be better off dead?"

"No," said Charlie D. "But if I did, I think I'd put pills in his wine or something before I'd take a fire extinguisher and beat his head in. It was not a loving act, Nick. So where do you want me to hang this plant? Does it matter how high off the ground?"

"I'll take care of it," said Magaracz.

Roberta herself was quite eager to take it. Mothering sickly plants was a skill of hers.

"Don't water it now," the detective said to her. "I just watered it."

"I can see that," she said. "You overwater it. That's what's wrong with it. It's getting root rot."

"I'll just hang it here over your desk," said Magaracz.

"Shouldn't it be closer to the window?"

"Maybe, but I've got it all hung now. We'll just leave it here and see how it does."

"It's awfully high. How can I ever reach it?"

"That's okay," said Magaracz. "Just call me when it's time to water it." He turned the tape recorder on and went out.

Charlie D. changed the tapes randomly when Roberta went on breaks or to the ladies' room. The tapes had an episodic quality, stopping sometimes in the middle of a sentence. Easy-listening music from Roberta's radio could be heard throughout.

Only now had Magaracz begun to listen to these

103

tapes, on his way home in a great crush of traffic from Atlantic City. It was the first really warm day of spring. It seemed that everyone who could get away had gone to the shore, and now they were all headed home again, crammed onto this single roadway. As Magaracz's car crawled through the South Jersey night he thrust the cassettes into the tape player one by one, straining to find some important clue, failing, ejecting, loading the next tape. In the dark the office noises sounded disembodied and oddly intimate. He should have heard the tapes coming down, he decided, in the daylight. They would have sounded more normal.

Of course at that time he had been studying Joe Piscione's two-volume cassette course entitled "Winning Ways at Blackjack."

The first two sides were of typing, pages rattling, file drawers opening and closing, telephone calls for Delpietro (which, once transferred to his phone, Magaracz could not hear) and, now and then, the sound of a fingernail file.

Eject. Jam the tape in. On.

Ten minutes of typing. The phone rang twice. Paper rustled.

"Good morning. Mr. Delpietro's office."

As with all the telephone conversations, the voice on the other end was audible only as a kind of buzzing.

"Alison. Hi. What's new?"

Buzz.

"With me? I don't know. Gee. When was the last time we talked? There was a murder up here a couple of days ago, but aside from that nothing much."

"Yeah. A murder. Didn't you see the papers? Someone killed an old man in the hall. It was horrible. They still haven't replaced the rug."

"No, Barry's not back yet. Miss him? I'm going crazy."

Buzz.

"I know. Alison, I did a really dumb thing the other night. I went to bed with this guy from the office."

Buzz.

"Charlie D.? (Giggle.) God, no. No, this one is real old and everything. He must be at least fifty. No, that would be real fun, getting it on with Charlie D. It wasn't anything like that."

"I don't know. I don't know what I did it for. It was, like, this guy's brother was just killed, the old man I told you about, and he was a complete wreck. I just felt so sorry for him."

"I don't know. It seemed to take his mind off things. It made me feel good, you know? To be able to affect another person that much. I just felt . . ."

Buzz.

"Not really. He's one of those guys that comes in three seconds and then apologizes for half an hour. He kept talking about Sheila."

"His wife."

Buzz.

"Oh, God, I hope not. What if he does want to? I just don't know, Alison. Like I said, it was really dumb. I guess if he does I'll just break it off somehow. God. He isn't even *cute*."

"Okay. Look, I have to go now, but why don't we have lunch tomorrow?"

Buzz.

"Good. See you then. 'Bye."

The receiver was laid in its cradle. The easy-listening music droned on.

This was not what Magaracz expected.

Four cars ahead of him, if only he knew it, Freddy and Angela were stuck in the same traffic jam.

She was still mad at him for gambling away her pay. If only he could be steady, instead of acting like some kind of a jerky kid. If only he could be fatherly. Honestly, sometimes she felt older than he was, even though there was ten years' difference in their ages. But she kept these reflections to herself and stared out the window.

Freddy, for his part, was coming down off the high that he had felt in the casino. His mood was swinging to one of dissatisfaction with the state of things. He decided to attack Angela, so quiet in her corner.

"How come you wear your clothes so tight, kid?" he said to her. "That dress looks really cheap on you. I mean, I like tight clothes on a woman, babe, but that dress is too tight."

"It didn't use to be this tight," she said.

"What're you, getting fat now?" He leaned over and pinched her belly.

"Freddy, I'm pregnant," she said.

In the adjacent line of traffic a small space opened up. Freddy swung the van into it, giving the finger when another driver sounded his horn. "This radio station sucks," he said. "Let's have some good sounds." He put on a tape and turned the volume up.

106

The Stones blared. He began to drum in time on the steering wheel.

"Freddy, what are we going to do?"

"We'll go back to my place," he said.

"Not tonight, Freddy, my mother's expecting me home."

"Come on. I got some tapes for the video recorder. We can take pictures while we make poosha-poosh."

"Freddy, I already told you I don't want to do that."

"Why not? You have a beautiful body. We could make some very exciting tapes. You should do it now, before you get all big and fat and covered with stretch marks." He saw that she was crying. "Shit," he said. "Crying again. Everything makes you cry. Death, birth, sex, everything. Cut it out, can't you?"

"Freddy," she said, sniffing, "are we going to get married or what?"

"Married?" he said. "Me? You?"

"Yeah, you and me. Us. Married." *Mrs. Weasel*, said a small voice in the back of her mind.

To her surprise he said, "Okay." And then, "Tomorrow. We'll get married tomorrow. Jesus, I wish I had some weed."

"In Maryland?" she pressed. "We could drive to Maryland. We could go right now. I had an aunt who got married in Elkton like that. They were very happy."

"We're not dressed for it. You can't get married in a skin-tight red satin dress."

"We could stop off home and change our clothes."

"Okay," he said. "Right. I'll drop you off, and you

107

can change your clothes, and then I'll go to my place and pick up a couple of things. And then I'll come back for you."

"Okay." She blew her nose. "We'll call in work and tell them we're taking personal days."

"Personal days. Right."

"We have to have some kind of honeymoon, right?" she said.

"Right, babe."

"As soon as I get home I'll tell my mother. If she's awake. I know she'll be happy for me. She'll see we're really in love. I know she won't say any more mean things about you."

"Right."

"Give me a kiss, huh?"

"I have to drive right now," he said.

Side number seven. Magaracz jammed it into the tape player as he sailed along a stretch of straight, empty road through the pine barrens. Spring streamed in through the vent windows, and he thought, *Soon I'll be home.* He daydreamed through the sound of office machines, thinking of how to tell Ethel he had lost the fifty dollars.

Stan Green's voice, softly apologetic:

"Roberta, can we talk?"

"Oh, hi, Stan. Sure."

"Roberta, darling, I told Sheila last night about us."

A small silence, then a small, cold voice: "Us?"

"She won't let me go. She . . . Roberta, will you be my mistress? It seems this is all I can offer you. Sheila was . . . She was . . ."

"Stan . . ." A deep sigh, of — passion? Annoyance? "Stanley, the other night . . ."

"Darling, the other night was the most wonderful night of my life. And the most terrible. The most wonderful and terrible."

"Yes, Stan, yes, but tonight I have to go play racquetball, and tomorrow Barry will be getting back from Houston —"

"Racquetball?"

"I'm sorry, Stan. What I'm trying to say is, I don't think we should see each other anymore."

"But —"

"Barry would be very, very deeply hurt."

"I see." Sound of two left feet, stumbling out of the office.

Another sigh, followed by muttering: "Told Sheila about *us*. You incredible *twit*." Sound of something banging on the desk. "Pathetic." Furious typing.

Magaracz was nonplussed. His witness had vanished, his fifty dollars was gone, and his chief suspects were not, after all, working together. He backed up the tape and played the exchange over again.

"Pathetic," Roberta's voice repeated.

Well, then . . . No, it would still work: what if Roberta wasn't in on it, but Green set it all up, did it all in the hope of . . .

Or maybe Eunice Fogarty did it. Outraged at the influx of loonies that was disturbing her office routine, Eunice took the fire extinguisher . . .

Magaracz drove on into the night, thinking, placing his suspects against the crimes in question like ill-fitting puzzle pieces.

Finally he put the blackjack tape back in and listened to it again, hoping to determine where he had gone wrong.

Among the citizens of Atlantic City who had been supplanted by the casinos was an old couple named Sam and Ada Feld. The Felds used to run a Mom-and-Pop grocery not far from the beach, and they did a good business in white bread, Pepsi, lunch meat, and Ring Dings, as well as the various other necessities of the New Jersey diet. But Royal Cosmic Casinos wanted their location.

There wasn't much choice for the Felds. They had to sell. Royal Cosmic offered them a great deal of money for their little home with the store underneath, and assured them that if they didn't take it, their lives would become unpleasant. They didn't like giving up the store, but Ada's knees were bothering her more and more, and Sam was perhaps getting too old to schlepp the stock.

They had a son with a family in Princeton Township. He suggested they might like to live in one of the attractive garden apartments near his housing development. They would be nearby for family dinners and babysitting, and there would be no more worries about keeping up a house. The more they thought about it, the better the elder Felds liked the idea.

After surveying the many choice apartments in the area, the Felds signed a long lease on four rooms and a kitchen underneath Freddy the Weasel Gruver. How many times they came to rue the day.

The Felds had not lived there a week before their airy apartment with its brand new kitchen and southern exposure became a hellish prison. Gruver, they discovered, was a rock fan.

Not your love-and-peace hippie rock fan, either. Not for Freddy Gruver the business of clamping on the old stereo headphones and enjoying his favorite sounds in stoned and blissful solitude. No. Gruver was vain about his stereo equipment, and eager to share the delights of his woofers and superpowered midranges with all mankind, or at least everyone within a three-mile radius. An atomic rock fan was he, and the unhappy Felds were living at ground zero.

None of the neighbors liked it, not even the young ones; at times five or six of them would be standing under Gruver's balcony in their nightclothes, yelling and chanting at him to stop the noise. To no effect.

The sound of the bass went straight into the frame of the building from whatever satanic engines Gruver used for speakers, and came out the walls and ceiling and even the floor. There was no defense against it. Useless to plug up their ears; the vibrations still rattled the Felds' upper plates.

The police wouldn't come. They didn't regard it as a serious enough nuisance. The building super was unresponsive, if not stiff drunk. Still there were many weekends when Gruver did not come home.

"Maybe he's dead," the Felds would sigh hopefully, and Ada would cook something nice and settle down to watch Lawrence Welk.

Last weekend Lawrence had been about five minutes into his show when Gruver came home and started up. Ada had a heart attack right in her chair. It was nothing but aggravation. She so loved Lawrence Welk.

Now the poor old lady was in the hospital, resting comfortably, and though she was out of intensive care and getting better every day, still Sam had to come home to an empty apartment and *bumpa*, *bumpa*, *bumpa*.

Tonight Gruver wasn't home. Somewhere, Sam Feld reflected, as he gazed unseeing at Johnny Carson's opening monologue, somewhere out there Freddy the Weasel Gruver was driving his van around the dangerous roads of New Jersey. Please, God, with all the young people who die in traffic accidents these days, why not let one of them be Freddy? Such a little thing to ask.

The van drove in. Sam Feld recognized the sound of the engine; his hearing was still keen enough for that even after all these months of pounding. He imagined rather than heard the tread of Gruver's Adidas-clad feet on the iron stairs. He heard the click of Gruver's lock and the door opening. Then he experienced the bone-jarring din of Gruver's speakers.

Another night of it.

But then, thought Sam, perhaps this night was different, for it seemed to him that he heard scuffling noises and actual thumps on the floor. Strange. Maybe Gruver had brought friends home with him. The thumps stopped; the rock and roll continued; incredibly, the sound of a chain saw began.

112

Now he cuts wood, thought Sam.

On and on the noise went, louder and even louder, until someone screamed out, "Waterbed!," the lights dimmed and came up, and all sounds stopped together. Was it the last line of a song? Sam sighed, waiting for the next record to begin.

Yet there was no next record; scuffles and bumps only, and then silence. Or almost silence. There was a sound — slow, rhythmic, steady — a sound of dripping. But it was soothing, and such a relief that instead of going to locate the source of it Sam sat and read a book.

When he went in to go to bed he found it. Pink water was dripping down.

11

LITTLE ANGELA waited all night, but her lover never came for her.

In the morning her mother found her sitting at the kitchen table, grim-faced, hard-eyed, smoking. As Deirdre went to get their morning bacon, her daughter said to her, "Mom, I took the checks."

"What checks? What are you saying?"

"It was me and Freddy. Mom, I'm pregnant."

"Oh, baby," said Deirdre, herself sitting down, felled before she reached the refrigerator. "Are you sure?"

"I'm sure, Mom. I got one of those kits. We were going to elope last night. He was going to pick me up."

"Where is he?" Deirdre said. Angela ground her cigarette out in the overflowing ashtray, ran her hands through her hair, and lit another. "That's not good for the baby, you know," her mother said.

"I don't know where he is," Angela said. "Philly, probably. Las Vegas. California. He sure isn't here, is he? I've been stood up. He's no good, Mom. I can see that now. You were right about him. He never was any good. I must have been out of my mind."

"Oh, Angie."

"What am I going to do?"

"First of all," said her mother, "get your hair out of your eyes. It'll be all right. Everything will be okay." She put her arm around the girl. "I'll stay home and mind the baby. I'll retire. I'll be eligible for early retirement in a few months." She spoke without thinking, as if these were old plans she had made once and put away for an emergency. But even as she spoke, pictures formed in her mind of herself with a little baby again, diapering it, taking it for walks, wheeling it through the supermarket. The baby would be like Angela. She had been a wonderful baby, sleeping through the night almost at once, smiling all the time, full of dimples, never a bit of trouble. "I'll take care of the baby, honey," she said again. "It'll be okay."

"But the checks."

"The checks that you and Freddy took."

"Yes, you know, the checks that the police and everybody are looking for."

"Where did you put them? Why ever did you take them?"

She chewed her hair. "I dunno. He dared me to, after I let him know you told me the combination to the safe. I must have been crazy."

"Why did I do that?" said Deirdre. "I never should have told you that. I blame myself."

"Oh, come on, Mom. That's silly. Anyway, we hid them at the office, and if he didn't take them they're still there.

"If he didn't take them and run off someplace, leav-

115

ing me flat, which would be just like him. The rat. How could I be so dumb?"

"Oh, baby, you're just young. Everybody makes mistakes."

"What am I going to do?"

"Give them to me, sweetie. I'll get my girls on the fourth floor to mail them out."

"Mail them?"

"Sure, honey. There's a new batch going out today. I'll just put the others in with them and it will be like nothing happened. Everyone will think they were lost in the mail all this time somehow."

"They're in the elevator tower under a floorboard."

"Leave everything to me," said her mother.

It was hours after dawn before the police were called to Freddy Gruver's apartment. As long as he made no noise, nobody wanted to complain about the Weasel. In any case, the super was not available for complaints during what he considered to be his own time. The tenants claimed that he customarily spent these hours (from 8:30 P.M. to 10 A.M.) in a drunken stupor.

Sam Feld was able to raise him at nine on Friday morning, by means of hammering and screaming, to report three hundred gallons of strangely colored water in his bedroom, and not without a certain amount of satisfaction. Feld considered that it broke his lease.

The super let himself in, saw at once that something was very wrong, and called the police. By ten o'clock the detective in charge of the case (another cousin of

116

Ethel's) happened to remember that Magaracz was working on something at the victim's place of employment. He telephoned him, because the family takes care of its own, even non-Italian in-laws. Magaracz arrived in time to see the police van driving away with the body.

Nothing of Freddy Gruver was left in the apartment but his many possessions, some stains, and a shapeless chalk line.

"Your fellow state worker, there, was tortured to death, it looks like," said the cousin, one Detective Guido Rosa. "Any ideas how come, Nick?"

"For laughs, maybe," said Magaracz. "Or information."

"In my experience," Rosa said, "guys torture women for laughs. Men they torture for information. As a general rule."

"What do you think?" said Magaracz. "Did he tell them what they wanted to know?"

"Personally, I would have told them, if it was me," Detective Rosa said. "You should have seen the body, Nick. Burns under the fingernails and the whole bit. Anyway, you're welcome to have a look around now that our boys are finished, before we padlock it. Maybe we can help each other."

"Any fingerprints?"

"Tons," said Rosa. "If we ever get the cuffs on the hands that go with those fingers we can put somebody away for a long time."

"What's on these videotapes?" Magaracz said, as he began to prowl through the wreckage.

117

"I don't know. Suppose we have a look."

At first the tape that was in the machine showed sequences of a self-conscious young woman in frilly underwear, trying to pose in the manner of a *Playboy* centerfold. The sound was of bits and snatches of rock music, and faintly in the background Freddy the Weasel murmuring encouragement. Rosa was greatly entertained.

Magaracz admired the video equipment. "If only I had something like this five years ago," he said. "Three years, even. It would have been really helpful in my work."

"I bet," said Rosa. "Say, who the hell is that?"

A young man had appeared on the screen, clipping his nails. He glared out at them and said, "I could get an apartment like this anytime I want." The camera zoomed in on him and then the screen went dark.

"Back it up, Guido," said Magaracz. He did, and played it again, stopping the tape at the last tight closeup.

"Hey, Mac, get over here and see if you can get a picture of this," Rosa called to the police cameraman, who was packing his things.

"I know that face," Magaracz said. "This guy was in the building the day the bookkeeper went out the window. Ten witnesses saw him, and another fellow with him."

"Our killer," said Rosa. "I'll bet you any money. Wonder if he knows what a nice picture of himself he left behind. Hot damn. Pack up that cassette with the other evidence, will you, Mac?"

118

"All you have to do is find him," said Magaracz.

"No problem," said Rosa, rubbing his hands. "We'll just paper Mercer County with eight-by-ten glossies. We've even got his fingernails, you know. He left them in that ashtray."

"Yeah, but who is he?" Magaracz said. And who was he going after next? That was the thing.

He went home for lunch. Ethel made spaghetti and meatballs. They were very good. He told her all about the latest developments in his case, leaving out the torture part so as not to upset her unduly. It would be in the paper anyway.

His delicious meal turned to a lump of lead in his stomach when she said, "Don't you think he'll go after Freddy's girlfriend next?"

Of course. Why hadn't he thought of that? He called the office but nobody answered. They were all out to lunch. He got in his car and headed for town at top speed. On the way there was an accident ahead of him and traffic was tied up. He turned on the radio. The news was full of Freddy's murder. They called it a probable gangland killing.

12

As it happened, Freddy had taken his secrets to his death, not because he was noble but because Junior's unfortunate accident with the ungrounded chain saw had prematurely terminated their interview. Freddy's accomplice and the whereabouts of Junior's checks were still unknown to the two brothers.

They wasted half the night trying to find a drugstore open where they could buy ointment and bandages for Junior's hand. He had huge blisters, and he was in a lot of pain. Liquor helped — luckily they had remembered to grab a couple of bottles on their way out of Gruver's dark apartment, so they didn't have to search for that — but by the time they were holed up for the rest of the night in a local motel Junior was getting very ugly.

"We gotta think," said Hanky to his brother, who sat on his bed, hugging his knees and rocking.

"About what?"

"If we just think of a good plan, we can find the checks and get back to Atlantic City. We'll be safe there."

"So think," said Junior, sucking his unhurt hand.

"The guy said his girlfriend got the checks for him, right?"

"Right."

"Only we don't know who she is."

"Right."

"Except we know she knows how to open the safe, right?"

"Right."

"And also we know she's probably a great-looking girl, like all those ones that he took the videotapes of."

"Sure, sure. What about it? You want to go up to the office tomorrow, round up all the great-looking girls, and ask them which one knows how to open the safe?"

Hanky was quiet for a minute. "No," he said, "but we could tell them there was a bomb in the safe, and then the one who opened it . . ."

By Friday afternoon it was all over the office that Freddy the Weasel Gruver had been brutally murdered on Thursday night. Angela was completely grief-stricken. Dead, her Freddy seemed like the world's most wonderful man. She had wronged him. Of course he would have come for her. They would be husband and wife right now, if only he hadn't been cruelly killed. She remembered the good times up in the elevator tower, times so sweet that even now the smell of machine oil was almost unbearably erotic. She had called it their house, and joked about buying a rug and curtains, even though there weren't any windows.

It was too sad. She couldn't even stand to go on

break with the women, but sat at her desk, using up Kleenex, balancing out the *Dedicated Unclaimed Journal*.

Eunice was right. You could find a lot of consolation in your work.

Presently she heard strange voices, and looked up through the open door to see the two men who had crashed Muriel's party standing over Roberta's desk.

"We need to get into your safe right away," one of them was saying. Sure enough, the bookkeepers had closed the safe door on their way to Janine's, forgetting that Angela was going to stay behind and work.

Roberta stared at the men. "Who are you?" she said. "What do you mean, you have to get into our safe?"

"Ma'am," said the one with the moustache, "we're police officers. Bomb squad. There's no time to lose."

They actually grabbed her arms and dragged her into the bookkeepers' office, where they stood her in front of the safe. "Go on, open it," one of them said. "There's a bomb in the safe set to go off three minutes from now."

"We have to disarm it right away," said the other one. "It will take us fifteen minutes just to get out of this building. By that time we'll all be dead."

"What are you talking about? I can't open this thing!" Stan Green came in. "Stan!" she sobbed. "Open the safe for these men!"

"I'm afraid I don't know the combination," he said. "Where's Eunice? What seems to be the trouble?"

"Bomb in the safe, sir," said the man with the bandaged hand. "Is there anyone on this floor who can open that safe? We only have two minutes now."

Green paled and began to wring his thin hands. Roberta was weeping loudly.

Angela stood up. "I can open it," she said. "Here, let me." She twirled the dial, worked the combination, and opened the safe with a clang.

There was nothing unusual in it.

They all stared at each other.

"Good work, honey. You're a real heroine," said Moustache.

"But there's no —"

"Let's go," said Bandage.

"Where?"

"We're going to take you downtown, and give you a medal. But first you show us where you put those checks." It was then that she felt the gun in her side.

Outside in the afternoon sun, Magaracz, approaching the office, noticed a new loony. She was standing in front of Woolworth's, gazing at her reflection in the window, wearing such an outfit as had not graced the streets of Trenton since the early sixties. A symphony in pink she was; pink jacket, tiny pink skirt, pink and white vinyl boots with the toes out, all crowned with a luxuriance of honey-colored plastic hair falling to her shoulders. Yet there was something familiar about the varicosed knees peeping under the miniskirt, as she turned and began to move toward him with that lurching gait, and he saw the two pairs of glasses . . .

"Hiya, honey, how do you like my new look?"

It was Ruth Ann Walker.

"Miz Walker!" Magaracz said.

"Oh, honey, I let all the handsome men call me Ruth Ann. Would you like to go to bed?"

"Another time, maybe. Ruth Ann, I have to talk to you. I've been looking everywhere for you, you know that? We even broadcast your description on TV."

"They don't have TV where I've been," she said, turning to her image in Janine's window to adjust her front teeth. "And, of course, if I can't fit one into my shopping bag, I don't own it, do I? Would you like to buy one of my hats?"

"Where have you been?" asked Magaracz. "Were you in Atlantic City?"

"Atlantic City? Oh, no, honey, I was in New York City. This spell of cold weather we've been having is bad for my Arthur Rightis. I thought I'd go and stay in the steam tunnels."

"Steam tunnels?" said Magaracz.

"You know. Down under the railroad station. It's kind of nice, if you like steam. Do you have a cigarette?" She turned to her reflection in the glass and wiggled her front tooth. "That's better. They come loose sometimes." Inside Janine's, Magaracz could see the bookkeepers having their afternoon tea. Good. That meant that Angela was safe. But, no; she wasn't with them.

Eunice Fogarty looked up and saw Ruth Ann. She said something to Rose, and the two of them came rushing out Janine's front door. "Mr. Magaracz!" said Eunice. "You found our friend Ruth Ann! How are you, dear? You're looking wonderful."

Angela led the men to the elevator tower. A blast of machine oil smell. Their blanket, still folded and waiting in the corner. The little home that the husband would never return to. Dead. He was dead. He wasn't coming back.

"Okay, where are these checks? Hey, quit blubbering. Hanky, take her and hang her out over the elevator shaft. Then she'll tell us."

She was frightened of heights. Hanky grabbed her arm and began to pull her toward the shaft. She screamed, a good long loud one.

Stan Green appeared in the stairway. He shouted, "Hey!" in a threatening voice.

Junior shot him. He fell back down the stairs.

"I told you before!" Angela said. "They're under the floorboard!" She pointed. "There."

Junior lifted the loose floorboard. He and Hanky stood looking in the hole.

There was nothing there but a tiny corner of yellow bank paper, caught between two boards.

"Ruth Ann, I have to ask you something," said Magaracz. "Do you remember the day Leo was killed?"

"Sure."

"There was someone you saw running away in the hall, you said."

"Yeah, sure. The bug-eyed man."

"Would this be him?" Magaracz produced an eight-by-ten glossy made from the television screen at Freddy's apartment.

Ruth Ann squinted at it, first through both pairs of

glasses, then one pair, then over the tops of both. "No," she said. She raised her head and gazed into the middle distance. "No, I think *that's* him."

"What's him?" said Rose Petrowski. Ruth Ann pointed a bony finger.

"There," she said. "The one in the suit."

They looked where she was pointing, and sure enough, there went a man in a dark suit, into the front entrance of the Mental Rehab building.

"Come on," said Magaracz to the women, "let's go catch him." He took Ruth Ann's arm and rushed in, followed by Eunice and Rose. No one was in the lobby; the snack lady had taken a break, and the watchman was not in his chair. One of the elevators was waiting, open. The other, to judge by the needle on its dial, was nearly to the twelfth floor.

"Let's go," said Magaracz, dragging Ruth Ann Walker into the elevator. Eunice and Rose trotted after them. Slowly, with all the usual hesitations and shudders, the elevator began to climb.

On three it stopped. A young girl in heavy makeup stared at the four of them, vacantly, continuing to chew her gum. She did not board. She said, "You're going up, right?" Chomp, chomp.

"You shouldn't have pushed the up button, dear, if you wanted to go down," said Eunice. The doors closed. The slow ride continued.

As they passed five, something went wham! on the roof of the elevator car. Ruth Ann let out a yelp. The elevator stopped, but only for a moment. With a groan and a tremor it started up again.

"What now?" said Rose. "These elevators are the world's worst."

"Beats the hell out of me," said Magaracz.

"I remember I got stuck between floors on this one once," said Eunice, "with some young fellow from the records department. My goodness, he was frightened."

"What happened?" said Rose.

"Well, of course, they started it up again and we got off at the next floor. But it took them five or ten minutes. In the meantime I thought that poor young man would go crazy. He was pushing all the buttons like a wild thing. Mr. Magaracz, are you all right?"

"Well, yeah. Why?"

"There's blood on your ear," said Eunice.

He put his hand to his ear and it came away bloody. He stepped back and looked all around. There was a thin trickle of red coming through the trap-door crack on the elevator ceiling.

"Oh, geez," he said. "Stop this elevator." But they were at the twelfth floor, and so it stopped by itself.

13

FRANKLIN HAD NO clear plan in mind when he got on the elevator. He thought, *The boys are up there. They're going to get into more trouble, perhaps kill somebody else, almost surely get caught.* It might be that he could get them out of there before that happened, perhaps exert some kind of moral force. As the floors blinked past he composed speeches to lead them out by. "Come on, boys, it's time to go." Obediently they would drop what they were doing and come with him.

Or maybe not. Maybe they would stand there and whine at him. "Aw, Dad, we were having *fun*." Then what would he do?

From far up the shaft a shot rang out.

Six. Seven. Eight. Clanking and wheezing, the elevator continued upward. The tension became unbearable, and Franklin took another pill, some antidepressant from the pharmaceutical salesman's kit that would surely give him the tranquillity he needed to deal wisely with his sons. There was nothing to wash it down with but the dregs in his whiskey flask.

The elevator doors opened on the twelfth floor to reveal Stanley Green fainting in the arms of Roberta Schwartz, the two drenched with tears and blood. The sight scarcely had any meaning for Franklin. *Michelangelo's Pietà*, he thought. He stood and gazed at them as if they were marble.

The woman pointed up the stairs with a bloodied finger and said, "Up there." It seemed like a direction from God. He mounted the stairs.

He was floating. He couldn't feel his feet. The iron balustrade conveyed no impression to his fingers.

Their backs were to him, but it was the boys, all right. Even by the dim light of the caged bulb he knew their posture and the shape of their shoulders. They stood unmoving, staring at something on the floor, a hole in the floorboards. A railing at knee level separated them from the elevator works.

A young girl crouched on the floor, facing them. Slowly, imperceptibly almost, she inched backward toward the stairs. Franklin put his hand on the wall to keep himself from falling. His hand made a black smear on the wall but still he couldn't feel it. Odd. His sons still hadn't seen him.

"You fuckup," Junior was saying. "You stupid asshole."

"Oh, right," said Hanky. "I did everything."

"I seem to recall that this was your brilliant plan."

"Junior, it was your idea to come here. I'm not getting nothing out of this."

"And who said it was okay to plug a three-pronged saw into a two-pronged extension?" said Junior, waving his hand, all bandaged.

"Nobody told you to carve up the waterbed, Junior."

"You're a little asshole and a dumb fuckup."

"Maybe so. At least I ain't drunk, or a homicidal maniac."

Franklin saw Junior's gun hand come back and then whack! across the side of Hanky's face with the pistol barrel. Hanky staggered sideways, then turned and kicked his brother in the groin, doubling him over.

"Stop it," said Franklin, but it came out so soft that his voice was drowned by Junior's cursing. With some idea of stopping the fight, Franklin lurched toward them. Hanky stepped back out of his brother's reach. Junior charged. But he struck his father, who caught the railing behind his knees and went over.

The drug Franklin had taken was very powerful. Right to the end he felt nothing in particular, not even mild anxiety.

"They're up there. One of them has a gun. They were going to kill me." Angela explained all this to Magaracz, who was fixing the bloody elevator so that it wouldn't move.

"Okay, it's all right now. Look," he said to the others, "I want all you ladies to go back in the far office, close and lock the door, and get behind the desks. Can you do that?"

"You bet," said Rose.

"I can't leave Stanley," said Roberta.

"Okay, then, the rest of you. Eunice, you call the police. Tell them about the gun."

"Right," said Eunice.

"And tell them to send an ambulance for Stanley."

Ruth Ann rolled her eyes and fluttered her big hands. "Police!" she said. "Say, I just thought of something important. I'm supposed to be someplace right now." She started down the stairs, clutching her shopping bag. "In fact, I'm late already." She was gone.

The others rushed to the back room. Magaracz heard the lock click. Now, what to do about these two? Roberta gazed at him with pleading eyes.

"How bad is he, Mr. Magaracz?" she said. He was certainly a mess, with blood all over his face like that. But, how bad?

"I don't know," Magaracz said. "What happened to him?"

"They shot him. He fell down the stairs."

How bad was he? Well, was he dead? Magaracz crouched down and peeled back an eyelid.

"Ow. Stop that," Stan Green said.

"'Scuse me," said Magaracz. "Look, Stanley, do you think you can move?"

Green moaned.

"Will he die?" Roberta whispered. "How long has he got?"

"Wait a minute," Magaracz said. Someone was coming down the stairs.

For a long time the boys stood, stupefied, and stared down the elevator shaft. "Who was that? Where the hell did he come from?" said Hanky. But Junior knew; it had happened to him before in a dream. Sprawled supine on top of the elevator, the body rose up slowly

131

until it came into the light of the caged bulb. It was all broken.

"It's Dad," said Hanky. "Junior, you killed Dad."

"He fell," said Junior. "He was stoned."

"What?"

"He lost his balance. He was stoned, I said. He was stoned all the time, you stupid ass. Don't tell me you didn't know that."

"But . . ."

"I gotta get out of here," said Junior. He went down the stairs, holding the gun out in front of him.

Something hit him hard on the arm. It made him drop the gun. He half turned. Magaracz took hold of his bandaged hand and wrenched it around behind him in a hammerlock.

"Hey, let go! Hanky! Help!"

"Calm down, son," said Magaracz. He kicked the gun over to Roberta, where she sat holding Stan Green. "Pick that up," he said, "and if anyone else comes down, shoot him."

"Let go of me, cop," said Junior, "or I'll sue your ass for police brutality."

"I'm no cop," said Magaracz, "I'm a fuckin' state worker."

Hanky appeared at the foot of the stairs, dazed and bruised. "Can someone help my father?" he said. "He's on top of the elevator." They all stared at him.

Roberta pointed the gun at Hanky. "Him, Mr. Magaracz?" she said. "You want me to shoot that one?"

Magaracz shook his head and maneuvered himself close enough to reach out and take the gun from her.

"You boys sit there against the wall," he said, "and keep your hands on top of your heads. There's an ambulance on the way. Also the police."

And very shortly they arrived, along with Charlie Delpietro, fresh from the golf course.

14

WARM, STICKY BLOOD ran down between Roberta's fingers. *Oh, God*, she thought. *He's dying*. This must be how Ethel Kennedy felt.

The ambulance crew came down the stairs. "We'll take this one first," one of them said. "The other guy's gone. We can't help him." They prepared to load Stanley on the stretcher.

"I love you, Stan," she said to him.

He was conscious. "I love you, too," he said, and then, "I think my leg is broken."

They splinted the leg, and carefully, carefully they put him on the stretcher. "Au revoir, my dearest," he said. One of the ambulance attendants wiped his head. Under the blood was a small flesh wound.

"That doesn't look so bad," said Charlie Delpietro. "I think they just nicked you, fella. You'll be back here in a couple of weeks."

"I know," said Stan Green. He was pale but smiling. "It's my leg. My head is all right. It's just bleeding." They rolled him onto the elevator. The door closed.

"Cuts on the head bleed a lot," Charlie D. observed. "But they're not serious."

"You mean he's not dying?" Roberta said. For the first time she noticed what a mess her clothes were.

"My guess is, he'll be back when he gets out of traction. Three, four weeks at the most," Charlie D. said.

Almost to herself, she said, "He thinks I love him."

"I can see where he might have got that idea, Roberta. Here you were, holding his head and saying, 'I love you, I love you.'"

"Oh, God. I thought he was dying."

"No. Probably he'll outlive us all."

"What am I going to do?"

"Up to you, sweetheart," Delpietro said.

"Oh, God." She looked at her hands. "What a mess."

Magaracz came in. "Well, that's that," he said. "Your troubles are over, Charlie."

Delpietro said, "Nick, you probably think I'm some kind of an asshole, but I still don't know what's going on."

"I would never call you an asshole, Charlie," said Magaracz.

"Who were those guys?" Delpietro asked him. "And why were they in here shooting up the office?"

Magaracz said, "This whole crowd is from that nursing home in Atlantic City, the Boardwalk View. Eunice says the state will have to take over and run it now that there's nobody to manage the place, so the patients don't get thrown out of their beds. I hope they'll hire a decent cook, and clean up the kitchen."

135

"But what were they doing here?" Roberta said. "What did they want?"

Magaracz said, "They were after those missing checks. For some reason they thought somebody here stole them. Obviously they were wrong. Do you see any checks? I don't. Could be they were just lost in the mail. You know how the state mail works. Could be they'll be delivered tomorrow, right where they belong."

"And no more grief from the *Star-Ledger*," murmured Charlie D. "Nice, Nick. I hope you're right."

"Trust me," said Magaracz.

"You're not really an accountant, are you?" Roberta said to him.

"No," said Magaracz. "I'm a man of mystery."

"I've got to wash," she said. She went to the ladies' room.

"What's she going to do now?" Magaracz asked Delpietro.

"About what?"

"Stan Green."

Delpietro sighed. "Oh, hell. Probably she'll ask for a transfer to some other department. Too bad. She's a good kid. Hey, are those ladies all right in there?"

"Sure," said Magaracz. "They're sitting around talking about cooking recipes."

Outside in the orange sunlight of late afternoon Magaracz is heading home to Ethel. He will stop at Barbero's bakery and pick up some cannoli, maybe, so they can curl up with coffee after dinner and get fat.

He had a long private talk with Little Angela. She told him everything. He said to her that it was okay, but she should shut up about it forevermore. As far as Magaracz was concerned, he never heard a word of it, right? The checks were in the mail. End of story.

Thinking about the whole thing, though, he has to laugh. Freddy is her hero now. She plans to go to court and take his name, call the baby after him, and all that stuff. For the rest of her life she'll be telling the kid what a wonderful guy his father was. The Weasel will be a better father dead than he ever would have living.

The trees in the church cemetery are gorgeously in bloom. The lineup of bums on the steps is almost the same. Leo is gone, of course, but five more are in his place, Ruth Ann among them. In the distance Magaracz can hear the wreckers pulling down another building.

Maybe it isn't so bad, working for the state. Maybe Magaracz will reconsider. He heard they need detectives over in the Bureau of Taxation.